BOOK OF SHADOW

THE HAWTHORNE UNIVERSITY WITCH PREQUEL SERIES
BOOK 2

A.L. HAWKE

PHANTOM HEART, LLC

ISBN: 978-1-953919-87-8 (paperback)

ISBN: 978-1-953919-88-5 (hardcover)

ISBN: 978-1-953919-84-7 (ebook)

ISBN: 978-1-953919-95-3 (audiobook)

Library of Congress Control Number: 2025911852

This is a work of fiction. It comes directly from the author's imagination. Witchcraft is included to infuse a sense of realism to the novel, but in no way is it supposed to represent actual practicing witchcraft, witches, or the religion of Wicca or Thelema. Any satanic groups portrayed in this series are purely fictional and not intended to represent actual people or organization(s).

The book also includes fictitious names, characters, places, and incidents. Any public names are used solely for creative purposes. Any resemblance to actual people, living or dead, or to companies, institutions, or locales is entirely coincidental or accidental.

Line edited by Stephanie Marshall Ward

Proofread by Alexa B., alexabooks.wixsite.com/authors

Cover Design © 2025 by Brosedesignz

Published by Phantom Heart, LLC

27702 Crown Valley Pkwy, STE D4 #201

Ladera Ranch, CA 92694

Printed and bound in the United States of America

First printing 2025

Learn more about A.L. Hawke at www.alhawke.com

Correspondence: contact@alhawke.com

❀ Formatted with Vellum

1

THEATER

IN A SEA OF SMALL, INCONSPICUOUS CREAMY-WHITE HOMES, BACK-to-back along a quiet suburban street, my destination isn't hard to find. The house number is 666. But if that isn't disturbing enough, the distinctive facade of the two-story destination is painted black. Pitch black. Obsidian. Like a shroud of night over a clear blue sky. It seems to absorb bright light reflected off the surrounding white homes. I glance at my folded triple-A map on the passenger seat. Yep, this should be the place. The neighborhood doesn't look great either. The homes surrounding this small coffin-house have chipped paint, dented and cracked walls, trash strewn about their front yards, and dead grass. How do I let Alondra talk me into this stuff?

I climb narrow red brick steps and knock on the black door.

I hear laughter. So I knock harder.

"Yeah? What?" asks a girl, swinging the door open.

She looks like a gypsy with her pale blond hair tied back by a black bandana, strings of beads and necklaces around her neck, and baggy pants. She smiles lasciviously, checking me out from head to toe. Behind her, a man walks in, wearing only white underwear, smoking a joint. He's adding to an already thick cloud of pot smoke in the house.

"I'm looking for the doctor," I say. And that makes me cringe. How does *doctor* fit into any of this? But that's the instructions Alondra left me.

Hung on a scarlet wall behind the girl is a very large black tapestry of a goat, the Baphomet, in an upside-down pentagram. Dozens of candles are lit on tables and on the carpet, making all the smoke in the room seem to glow. Another woman walks by behind the gypsy. This one is pale with short black hair, wearing a thin black robe. I see the curves of her breasts under her robe.

"Who's there, Silvia?" asks the passerby.

"That fella meeting Lumi, Cline," she hollers back. She spins back toward me, still holding the door, grinning. "Hey. I'll tell the doctor you're in, okay? But...did you bring the book?"

I pat the old leather book under my arm. Apparently, the book is the entire reason Allie wanted me to visit.

"May I?" she asks, reaching for it.

It's weird, but Alondra left explicit instructions to not, under any circumstances, let anyone touch it. She just wanted me to come here and show it to them. So I shake my head.

"Hey, why the fuck not?" she asks, pouting. But she laughs. "Fuck it then." She spins around and cries, "Lumi! Hey, Lumes! Falconsong sent her High Priest."

"I'm not a High Priest."

"Sure you ain't," she says, glancing back with another big smile.

"Bring our guest into the living room, Silvia," announces a man with a British accent. "I'll be with our warlock in just a moment."

"I'm not a warlock."

She reaches for my hand. I don't give it to her, so she manages to snatch my elbow instead. Then she leads me past an open living room to my right and through another door.

This room, with those same scarlet walls, scented in sandal-wood and marijuana, has a very old ratty brown couch, two matching lounge chairs, and a fireplace. Above the couches, along the walls in the flickering candlelight, is a string of pentagrams and upside-down crosses scratched or marked in black ink. On the end table is a bunch of books—some appear to be as old as the one tucked under my arm—along with crystals, colored gems, animal bones, cards, and black wands. There's a distinctive large animal skull with horns on the marble hearth.

Silvia gestures for me to sit on the ratty brown sofa. I finally take off my heavy coat and lay it beside me. And then I sit down.

She plops down by my side.

"So, tell me," she says, "what's your coven like?" She lays a hand on my leg. I brush it away. "I hear," she says, looking up dreamily, "that the Hawthorne Witch is *sooo* powerful. I mean everyone, like everybody, knows Alondra. Our god is fond of her. I'd so like to attend one of her rituals."

"I wouldn't know. I don't attend her ceremonies."

"But you brought the book," she says, furrowing her brow. "And..." And she pats my hand. "That is like, totally, utterly cool. We have nine members in our group. Nine. But I'm fascinated by theurgy. Thirteen is amazing too. And your tradition of a female leader versus Lumi, our god, is absolutely fabulous. I love how you can create a religion in artful ways. It's far out, a'ight? That would be my preference for my order. I thought of joining a traditional coven once, you know, when I was little, but I mean wait, *I mean*, just you wait till you meet him. Lumi's totally the bomb. I tell you, he is da bomb. There is no better wizard in the whole wide world than our doctor. You'll see. But..." She scoots closer. "Hey...so, can I touch it now?"

"No."

"Why the fuck not?" she asks, leaning back with a frown.

"I was told not to let anyone touch it," I say with a laugh.

"Jeez, man, I mean just for a second. Lumi told me it's so powerful." Then she lifts her palm over it and closes her eyes.

"Okay, let me...I tell you what, keep it under your arm and just let me feel it from here for a sec. 'Kay?"

And that's really weird. But how is it any stranger than the house?

"Leave him alone, Silvia," warns that older girl with short hair in the black robe.

Cline comes over and hands me a white porcelain cup on a saucer. I can definitely tell she's not wearing clothes underneath her nearly translucent dark robe.

"Hey, fuck off, Cline," Silvia snaps at her. "You leave me the hell alone, 'kay? This guy is hella cute and he's got the book. Like, *the* book, Cline. *The* Book of Shadows. So...I mean, it's not often that we get a witch from another coven."

"I'm not a witch."

"Leave him alone or you're gonna get it, Nancy," Cline warns, raising her brow. "Remember what the doctor told you?"

"Fine," Silvia snaps, jumping up. "Well, nice meeting you." She reaches out to shake my hand. "By the way, what's your name?"

"Liam."

"In our order, I go by Silvia. But you can call me Nancy. Or you can call me Silvia. Or you can like, switch it up, and call me Silvia sometimes and Nancy others." She laughs. "I like both names."

"Nice meeting you, Silvia," I say with a chuckle.

"Sure." Then she turns to Cline. "Hey, he's cute, isn't he?"

"The doctor will be with you in a moment, Liam," Cline says. Then she pulls Silvia hard by the arm, and they start walking out of the room.

"What's this?" I ask, lifting the cup.

"Jasmine tea," Cline answers, already outside the room.

Then I'm left alone.

I cough. I worry I might get high just breathing in the smoky air.

The fireplace in the room is not just any fireplace. There's a wood table beside it with, of course, a crimson tablecloth. Atop the red cloth is a golden chalice and knife. I've learned enough from my girlfriend to know that this is a ritualistic altar. And on another table, on the opposite side, I see a wand, a whip, and a metal chain beside a smaller animal skull.

A tall middle-aged man with a goatee enters the room. He is pale-skinned and bald, wearing a cape with a red satin interior and a black robe underneath. He looks like a mix between a stage magician and Satan. Adorning his neck is a large, thick brown and green camouflaged snake.

"Please, stay seated," he says, putting his hand up. "I'm so happy to meet one of Alondra's good friends."

"You must be the doctor?"

Obviously.

He sits down on one of the beat-up lounge chairs across from me. Meanwhile, the large snake slithers slowly, revealing a black upside-down cross tattoo on his neck.

"I promised your High Priestess I'd visit your college one day," he says, petting his snake.

"You know Hawthorne University?"

"I've had some encounters with your High Priestess," he replies with a nod. "I met up with her in one of her hauntings with her ghost hunters." He chuckles. "We've even shared ceremony. Her craft is renowned throughout the South—the whole world, for that matter. And she's proved her power to me more than once. But...no, no, I've never been to your college."

He steeples his hands. Then he creepily examines me in the flickering candlelight.

"I heard rumors about your coven's fallout," Lucius says. "Of course, I knew of your High Priest's spellcasting. The former wizard of your coven was as feeble and simple-minded as Alondra is powerful and brilliant."

"Capper was an idiot."

Lucius slowly nods.

"Of course, the offer's tempting," he says with a sigh, "but...I can't understand why she doesn't pick you."

"Pick me? For what?"

"What do you mean, for what?" he asks, laughing. Then he points at the cup and saucer on my lap. "You can drink that. I assure you it's perfectly safe. Cline brews a delicious jasmine tea."

"I think you get my hesitation," I say, gesturing about the room.

No, he really doesn't. He furrows his brow, glancing about the room, seemingly confused.

"Ah, I see. Well, I am a magician, Liam. I suppose I've grown accustomed to the decorations in this house. All this is...shall we say, *theater*." He puts a finger to his chin, pensively rubbing his beard. "All ritual is theater. A show to draw power within— our magical intent—to cast spells and do what people call magic. Aleister Crowley called it ritual magic with a "k." My magic is very real, but all these symbols help draw the circle's energy. But these things—" He looks about and chuckles again. "Incense, smoke, sigils, our altar under Baphomet, is merely symbolism. Nothing more." He leans forward. "It's what it does *inside* of you that's important. But why should I tell you? You're being taught by one of the greatest witches of all time."

We're interrupted by Cline, who walks into the room again and takes a knee before him. Then she bows her head deeply, offering him a fresh cup with a saucer. His cup is steaming, and the way she's presenting his tea with both hands it looks like she's offering a sacrifice.

"Hail, Satan," she whispers as he takes the cup from her hands.

"Hail Satan, my blessed Androgyne," he answers, patting the top of her head. "Blessed be, empress." She cocks her head back and smiles at me. Then Cline rises from her knees and exits the room.

He sips his tea.

"Theater, Liam," he repeats. "Simply theater. All life is theater."

"But our lives aren't rituals."

"No, no, that is not true. Every moment of your existence is a ritual. My order has discovered that the greatest experience, even greater than spellcasting, comes from breaking your resistance from within. Everything you've learned since you were born has imprisoned your soul. Society refers to everything in my house as the enemy? Is Satan your adversary? Think harder. Perhaps society's gods, their one god, the demiurge—Yaldabaoth, as the Gnostics called him—is our true enemy? And darkness by the light of Lucifer might be your true salvation? What would you say to that?"

He pauses to pet his snake.

Honestly? I'm about ready to jump up and run out of the room—after I complete Alondra's weird mission. I have yet to show him the book.

"The true answer to gnosis is the breaking of your chains. This is what Crowley taught when he instructed his disciples to believe in one thing, do the opposite, counter it, and do the contrary. Such disorder builds spirit. This is the result of the ritual of Abramelin in meeting Choronzon, facing your guardian angel, your demons, or your shadow, and relinquishing your ego and passing over the abyss of D'at into the blessed realms above. Chaos magicians believe in breaking order by conjuring disorder. I decorate my home to remind me of this chaos, a fight with my thoughts, until the blessed scarlet harlot, our revered Babalon, the blessed whore, one day graces me with her presence. Or..." He shrugs, sips some tea, and then runs his fingers along his thick snake again. "I await such abyss upon my death. Either way, it shall one day be revealed to me. Understanding this divine gnosis is very much like the salty taste of blood gliding over skin cut by an athame. Is it not? Such rituals lead to gnosis and salvation. Said more simply:

Ninety-three, ninety-three, ninety-three, and blessed be, warlock."

Then he pauses and sips more tea.

I stand up.

"Observing you," he says, pointing a finger and squinting, "I believe Alondra shouldn't be sending me the message. She should be delivering it to you, young man."

"I think I should be going. I'm not a witch or warlock, sir. I don't even practice witchcraft. I'm just a friend of Alondra's. I was told to show you the book. So, here it is." I flash the book toward him. "Now that it's getting late, I really need to head back home to Hawthorne—"

"May I see it?" he asks, reaching for it.

"No, she said you can't touch it."

"Please, sit. You are my guest."

I shake my head.

He jumps up. I'm surprised by his vitality. For a middle-aged man, his reflexes surprise me. Then he snatches the book out of my hand before I can stop him.

"Give it back," I warn. "Alondra said no one can touch it."

"*Broomstick?*" he asks with eyes wide open, shaking his head and staring at the book. He falls back into his chair with the book in his lap. "*Broomstick?* What a silly moniker Alondra gave it. It's hardly a broom. Nor is it a wand. But it is a tool, isn't it? Perhaps an instrument to wipe away confusion and lead us to the light? Or an object to focus our intent? Like a chalice? Bringing only more power by my wand."

"I said, give it back, Lucius."

But he's way too enthralled to be paying attention to me.

"Fascinating workmanship. This book is said to have belonged to Escoba Hawthorne, Liam, but she was a voodoo Manbo. Such a Book of Shadows is more in line with the tradition of Celtic lunar worship, is it not? I wonder if the book had two witch owners? One voodoo, one Celtic? Falconsong naming this book *Broomstick* hardly does the work justice.

Typical of Alondra to take something so arcane and title it anserine."

"Hand it back now," I demand.

He raises an index finger. "Allow me to receive her message first."

"*Revelare*," he says, waving a palm over the book.

Pages quickly rush by, turned by some invisible force under his palm until it is midway through the book. Looking over his shoulder, I watch as one of the blank pages quickly fills with handwritten words. I recognize the scribbling as my girlfriend's handwriting, but I can't fully make out what Allie's saying.

He slams the book shut, rubs his beard, and nods slowly. Then he hands the book back to me.

But then, gazing at me, his eyes widen.

"Such magic doesn't surprise you, young man?"

"I've seen worse," I say with a shrug.

"I see." He nods very slowly. "I see. Indeed." Then he regains his smirk. "Your reaction's more convincing than the book. I wonder if Alondra realizes sending you was more convincing than her grimoire—she probably did. Thank you for delivering the message, warlock. Tell Alondra I accept her invitation."

2

HOMECOMING

"Lee!" Allie jumps into my arms. "Oh, Lee!" Then she sends kisses all over my face and lips. "Oh, Liam, I've missed you so much!" I barely get through the door before Alondra's totally making out with me under the crystal chandelier.

"Let me put my bags down," I say with a laugh.

"Nope, not done kissing you."

But finally she snatches my brown leather satchel from my hand.

"How was it, babe? Tell me everything. I so wish I could have gone with you. Bill kept telling me how fun Myrtle Beach is."

"I didn't go there. I just saw Mom in Raleigh."

We make our way down the hallway to "my room." Yep, this year, Allie convinced me to stay at her amazing house. Halfway down the hallway, we dodge our small black cat, Sheba. I reach out and pick her up.

"God, I mean, two weeks, Lee? Two weeks! What sort of a winter break was that? Well, Rachel and Holly are planning a birthday party for Beth. They keep asking me about Atlanta. We can probably celebrate there, but it'll be your birthday around the same time. There's a really nice place, remember?

That fancy vegetarian restaurant we went to on my birthday? It's got cashew salad. You can get soy burgers or something. But it's your birthday, so...I don't know. You tell me. Rachel was going to try to channel you in the fireplace and ask you, but I instructed her not to." Alondra laughs. (She's not joking.) "A few days ago, we all helped your friend move into his apartment. It's like you left Mr. Dullness to take your place."

"I can't believe Bill's transferring here," I say with a chuckle.

"He wants in on our circle. Honestly, I'm not sure I trust him. But...I think that's—" She opens the door to the guest room. The bedsheets are made on the white canopy bed, and a scented candle on the dresser is emitting oleander. "That's gotta be why."

She puts my satchel on the bed. Then she opens it, helping me unpack. She pulls out the ancient book *Broomstick*. And she just stares at it. You know, the book I presented to the "doctor." I tell you, this book is like a drug for her. I think she started unpacking the bag just to see if it was in there. Last year the witch council left it under my care. That nearly ended our relationship altogether.

She quickly hands the book back.

"So, whatcha think? Can we celebrate your birthday in Atlanta? Hey, why are you being so quiet?"

"It was a long drive, Allie."

She nods. But then she comes close, takes me in an embrace, and makes out with me again by the doorway.

"I missed you so much."

"Bill's excited," I say, pulling away gently. I open my duffel bag on the bed, bringing out a whole pile of shirts and pants. "Mr. Mundane, as you called him, really wants to learn from your coven."

"Yeah, well, Mr. Dullness just wants to be around girls. That's all."

"He's devoted to parapsychology," I reply, shaking my head.

"Yes. I respect him for that."

"I like what you did to the room."

"You do?"

That's when I decide to reach deep into my satchel and hand her a souvenir. It's a small aqua-blue velvet jewelry box. Her emerald eyes open wider than ever.

"Is this what I think it is, Lee!"

"No, no," I say, laughing and raising a hand. "It's not that."

"You never know. I might say yes."

She shakes the small jewelry box. Then she pulls off the white bow and opens the box. Inside is a small green emerald on a thin silver chain. I couldn't resist. North Carolina happens to be renowned for its deposits of emeralds, you know. But the real reason—the color of the gem totally matches my girl-friend's eyes.

"I love it! Come on, help me try it on." She spins around so her back is toward me. "I love it so much."

I unclasp the small chain and lay it around her pale neck. She turns and faces me with those gorgeous eyes that inspired the gift.

"Well?"

"Beautiful," I say, running my hand along her cheek. "It reminds me of your eyes."

She blinks demurely. And then she's right back to launching into my arms.

Somehow, we end up rolling on the bed, messing up those perfectly straightened sheets. She pulls off my shirt and rubs the bare skin and hair on my chest. And then she's back to kissing my lips, stroking my hair, and running her hand all over my stomach. Before I know it, my pants and underwear are down. Then she lifts up her shirt, revealing her naked breasts.

"Are we doing this now?" I ask with a laugh. "Shouldn't we go upstairs?"

"I've been missing you for so long," she says, leaning down and kissing my lips again. "I kept passing by your room. Don't leave me like that ever again."

And she starts groping between my legs.

"Allie, wait. Wait...wait just a second." I turn on my side. "I need to talk to you about that cult you sent me to. Your errand."

"You want to talk about that *now*?" We both laugh again. But then I can't reply, because she climbs back up to my face, covering my neck and cheeks with kisses again. "What do you want to know, handsome?"

"When you asked me to visit, I didn't expect a satanic cult."

"The house address was 666."

"Yeah, and his place was decorated like the pit of hell. And your so-called *doctor* looked like Satan."

"Actually, Lucius is a chaos magician."

"Yeah, well, there was enough smoke to make you think the house was on fire. Everyone was walking around with barely any clothes. Why did you want me to show him, of all people, the book? But then not let him touch it? I couldn't stop him from grabbing it, by the way. He took it right out of my hands and cast some spell. Then he said, "I accept." Accept *what*, Alondra?"

She's back to leaning toward my lips. I scoot back.

"Accept *what*, Alondra?"

I tilt her face up because she's gazing down at my legs. She sighs and glides her breasts slowly along my chest, arousing me more.

"You're kinda ruining the mood," she says.

"Accept..." I insist on lifting up her chin again. "What?"

"If I answer, will you fuck me?"

"I guess so."

She sits by my side and smiles, her eyes now matching the gem on her necklace.

"You've told me a million times that you want nothing to do with our witchcraft. Well, I told you that we would arrange, somehow, me being a witch and leaving you out of my coven. But in order for me to practice magic, I need thirteen witches. One of those thirteen witches, Liam, has to be a man. And it ain't ever gonna be Capper again. And it doesn't sound like it's going to be you. Right?"

"You're inviting a devil into the coven?" I ask, nodding.

"You're so smart, babe," she says, lightly slapping my shoulder.

"That's not funny."

She leans down to kiss my lips again, but I gently push her off.

"You can't. We agreed to keep me out of the coven, sure, but we also agreed that you would stop practicing satanic witchcraft."

"Now hold on a minute, Liam," she says, turning mad for the first time. She sits up straight and throws her hair back. "When we made up, you said that I would stop doing satanic ceremonies. But we never agreed that I wouldn't associate myself with warlocks who practice that stuff. That's asking way too much."

"Allie, this man is everything Kenosha accused you of being."

"Wow," she says, "you're sure messing up the mood."

She falls on her back, heaving a sigh. Then she stares up at the ceiling. I catch her playing with the small emerald on her neck between her fingers. She closes her eyes. All the while, I watch her naked breasts move slowly up and down. The whole thing is arousing as hell, and I know her well enough to know that she's teasing me. She knows I'm watching.

"Emeralds harness the heart chakra," she says, closing her eyes tightly. "It's the perfect gift for us tonight. Not to mention," she adds, turning to me, "it shows me how much you adore me."

"I love you, Alondra."

"Well, I love you to death. But you have to accept what I am. The man I asked you to visit is the most powerful warlock in the world. If you spent enough time with him—which I'm sure you didn't—he'd explain to you that he doesn't believe in God.

He's an atheist. He challenges your norms and uses symbols against your god to provoke your mind. But I'm not going to get into philosophy and anti-Christian stuff, because you really don't care, do you? Right now, I just want to make love to you."

"Oh, Allie," I say, turning on my back and hitting my forehead. "I love you."

"You don't have to sound so upset about it," she says with a laugh. "Babe, just shut up about Lucius, a'ight? I love that you ran my little errand. Thanks. Now you seem tired. Why not rest? Really, it'd be wonderful just falling asleep in your arms. That'd be better than making love to you. But I don't get why you insist on sleeping down here all the time." She laughs. "We always end up upstairs in bed anyway."

"I don't want to rest."

"*Really?* My, my, what do you want to do instead then?"

I answer by turning to my side and running my hand over her breast. Then I touch her erect nipple as I touch my lips gently to hers.

"Umm," she says.

Our tongues dance. She wraps her arms around me, pulling me so close. And one of my hands strays down her leg and touches her side and then moves over her ass.

"I think you're casting a spell on me again," I say.

"One day you'll understand," she whispers between kisses, "that everything I am *is* a spell."

And isn't that what Lucius said? Everything in life is a ritual.

She rolls on top of me, still pressing her lips to mine. Below, her hand starts stroking my cock. I hear the tear of a condom wrapper. Then she rolls the condom on, moves over me, and repositions her body until I enter her.

Slowly, gently, she rides up and down as I feel the pleasure build. I squeeze her breasts. Her nipples are so hard, and the nape of her neck is starting to blush in the flickering candlelight. I'm ravenous. I mean, both of us seem unhinged after being apart for so long. If there's a spell, it's only amplifying our desire.

She moves up and down harder, faster. And then she moans. I squeeze her hips and ass, grasping her closer and squeezing her tight. Then my hands wander up and down, massaging the soft skin along her back until I reach the crack of her ass. She's stroking my cheek—my fuller beard that I didn't have a chance to shave on the trip. Then I feel those lips on my cheek, kissing me again.

I flip her on her back. She gasps in surprise, but laughs, opening those emerald jewels wide.

"That's it," she says. "Come deeper. Yes, deeper. Oh god, Lee, I love you...so much. I love you. And I missed you."

I start to fondle her breasts again, but she doesn't let me. Instead, she pulls my body tightly against hers. She's panting. So am I. I run my hand over her breasts again, then touch that new pendant with my fingers. I feel her heart pounding.

"Oh, fuck, Lee! That's it! Fuck me!"

Her body falls limp under me.

Then, quickly, her hands grope along my body to hold me. Her arms grip me so tightly in an embrace.

"Never let me go," she says. "Don't you ever, ever do that. Oh, I love you so much, Liam. I've never loved any man more than you. Don't be away like that ever, ever again. You hear?"

I turn on my side and hold her in my arms. And then I close my eyes, happy to just sleep with her beside me.

3

THE DIVINE FEMININE

THE LARGEST LECTURE HALL AT HAWTHORNE UNIVERSITY IS Drakewood Breyer Hall. They say over four hundred students can fit into all those black fold-out chairs. It's windowless, enclosed in drab dark brown walls with a large speaker hanging in each corner. Two side aisles and one central aisle slope down to a raised wood stage. There's another hall right next door that can be connected remotely through a video monitor. That one seats another hundred and fifty students. This is a huge lecture hall in a school that matriculates only around five thousand students per year. And it's the greatest hall for the greatest teacher at Hawthorne University, whom Alondra and I love: Dr. Kriegel. Professor Kriegel's a short, bald, stout guy who never dresses formally. He's always in sweatpants and a T-shirt. Right now he's rummaging through our textbook at the podium.

It's dark, as the lecture's about to start, with only the light from the projector screen shining behind him. Last year, when I was a freshman, Alondra and I attended his class on homicidal maniacs. When we heard about his occult class, there was no way we weren't going to take it together again.

"He told me he's got some big surprise," my friend Billy

says, sitting to my right, tapping a pen on a notepad. Bill's leaning back with his tennis shoes jutting into the right aisle. "The topic's something you and your lady friends would sure like. Numbers and witch covens."

"The class is Psychic Psychology and the Occult."

"Yeah, except *I* was supposed to teach about Sister Concezione and her devil letter this morning. Why are you taking this class, anyway? Is it because I'm the TA? Did you want me to grade you or something?"

"Alondra," I say with a shrug. "She might be a history major, but you know she wasn't going to resist joining me in a class on occult magic taught by our favorite teacher."

"Did you ask her yet about inviting me to her cult?"

"She said she thinks you just want to see her friends naked."

"Why not?" he asks with a laugh. "The girls in your club are hot. I don't mind as long as they don't mind seeing me au naturel."

"The circle disrobes out of respect for nature. I've left every ceremony before seeing them do it. I respect them for what they're doing."

"And I don't? I've been studying the supernatural and the occult longer than you. The fact is, your girlfriend can be a complete bitch. She knows how much I want in. If she excludes me then, Liam, well, I think I'm going to have to start hating her. But, hey, if she invites me...well...then all's forgiven. Anyway, when that invite comes, buddy, you should join too. The whole thing's so messed up. Your girlfriend's dying for you to join her, but you don't want to. I'm dying to join, but—"

"Ahem..."

Standing over Bill is this gorgeous girl in a black leather jacket, a brown silk button-down blouse, and black jeans, a black leather backpack slung over her right shoulder. The black clothes contrast with her pale complexion and perfectly match her soft dark hair, which flows down her shoulders. And her smile kills me—especially with her face made up like it is today. She's without gothic makeup, having chosen red lipstick instead. I love that.

As Billy lifts his legs, Alondra scoots across two desks to the open seat to my left. She plops down her backpack between her legs and pulls out books and pens. And then she does what I absolutely adore: She pulls the desk out from the fold-out chair and arranges a small notepad and two pens on it.

Finally, she turns to me and grins.

"Hi."

Billy smirks. He throws his legs back, blocking the aisle again.

"Hi, Alondra," he says gruffly.

Alondra leans toward me. "I'm a little nervous, babe," she mutters.

"Why?"

"Just wait and see, Lee," she says with a wink. Then she loses her smile, glancing over at my friend. "Hi, Bill."

"All right, everyone." Dr. Kriegel is walking from the podium to center stage. He's shadowed by the yellow light from the projector, still shining behind him, and his voice is amplified by the microphone. "This afternoon we're trying something a little different. I really want all of you to feel more like participants this semester. I hated structured didactics when I was in school. I felt as if there was always a wall between students and teachers. So, I'm excited to announce we're doing something a little different today. Today, I'm inviting one of your fellow students to come up and give a talk. I'm hoping to invite one or two others before the end of the semester. Each lecture counts as extra credit. I will review your subject and slides beforehand and, if approved, schedule you to talk. Of course, I think it's a wonderful opportunity to practice public speaking—particularly for those of you planning on making teaching a career."

He pauses and looks down for a moment. He's right over us.

Then he looks down at his teaching assistant next to me, my best friend Bill.

"During recent office hours, I spoke with a senior in your class who expressed a great deal of passion for the subject of stars and horoscopes. That led to an enlightening discourse over numbers."

"Wish me luck, babe," Alondra says by my ear.

"Please welcome Alondra Billington."

What... the... fuck?

The hall erupts in applause. It's loud because the whole lecture hall is packed. My mouth is gaping. And as Alondra walks up the aisle toward the stage, I catch Billy scowling. Boy, Bill's seething. Alondra and Bill seem to constantly be fighting. Still, I never would have thought they'd be competing over *lecturing*.

Alondra makes her way up to the podium, and Dr. Kriegel hands her the microphone. She attaches it to the collar of her blouse, under her jacket. Then she takes a notepad from her pants pocket and flips through a couple pages.

"Hi, everybody," my girlfriend says with a bright smile, waving.

"*You go, girl!*" cries a lady in the audience. I'm not sure who that is. Really, Alondra knows just about everyone on campus.

"This is such a great honor, professor," Alondra says, nodding to Dr. Kriegel. And then, just like her professor, Alondra takes center stage carrying only her small notepad in her left hand. She seems the exact opposite of what I would be under these circumstances. Confident.

She raises a remote in her hand and looks at the screen behind her. A slide reveals women with white flowers in their hair holding hands in a circle under the bright yellow sun.

"I've been asked to discuss the arrangement of witches in a coven relating to the number thirteen. Thirteen is a magic number. You will see that the number thirteen signifies not only the number of witches in a circle, but also the thirteen signs in the zodiac."

She pauses and glances down at her notebook. "Ready?" she asks, looking up at everybody with a big smirk.

The audience laughs.

"Okay... When Gerald Gardner founded Wicca, he chose this exact number, thirteen, for the number of witches that can make up a group, or coven, as he called it. Thirteen. This seemingly insignificant fact is glossed over by so many of us. Why did he choose the number thirteen? Isn't the number thirteen unlucky?"

She pauses and shakes her head. Then she looks down at Bill. Her smile widens. *Is she gloating?*

"Allow me to go over some basic numerology first. Numbers hold great power. They're magical. It's said that Nikola Tesla refused to stay in any hotel room without a number divisible by three. He knew of the power of three, six, and nine. The number three when multiplied by itself becomes the number nine. And the number nine is the most magical number in the world.

"Multiply any number by nine and you get nine. Try it. Three times nine is twenty-seven. In numerology, you add the digits together to get a single number. The sum of the two digits in twenty-seven, two and seven, is nine. In any example, adding the digits you get when multiplying nine by another number will result in nine. Nine times fifteen, nine times three-thousand six hundred. Nine times any number will always come to nine when you add the resulting digits. This same magic occurs with adding. The number added to nine will equal the number. For example, seven plus nine is sixteen—and one plus six equals seven.

"As an aside...in numerology, any number said three times —notice, *three*—focuses its magical power. So nine-nine-nine would be highly significant as the most magical occult number in the world. And, fascinatingly, like an upside-down cross, flipping those nines gives you—guess what? Six-six-six, a mockery of this positive spiritual energy. Not necessarily evil, though, because the sixes represent Earthly energy. Just like eleven-eleven or black and white. Anyway, back to nine."

But she pauses for a moment.

"Didn't think we'd be doing math this morning, did you?"

People laugh.

"Seven plus nine is sixteen and adding the two digits, one and six, gives you seven. The nine disappears with addition. So you see, with multiplication the numbers always equal nine, and with addition the number nine disappears from the final solution. Do you see the power of the number nine?"

No, not really. I think she's lost everybody. But it doesn't really matter because, like me, they love her mystery. Her mystery, her *occult*, is mesmerizing. And it's precisely why this lecture hall is packed with students studying Psychic Psychology and the Occult.

"I'll pause and let you eggheads try the calculations on a calculator. Go ahead. Try it and see what I mean... I'll wait."

And she waits.

In silence, we hear a chuckle or two as she just stands there mid-stage in her leather jacket and dark clothes gazing down in contemplation. The audience loves it. Then she saunters over to the podium and just gazes, with head held high, at the hundreds in the audience.

"Okay, what does this all have to do with the power of thirteen?"

She glances at her small notebook and then clicks on her remote toward the screen behind her.

A grisly picture of three witches burning at the stake lights up behind her. Everyone applauds like crazy. Because the grisly pictures are in homage to our favorite teacher, Dr. Kriegel. Dr. Kriegel loves planting zinger slides like this in all his lectures.

In the aisle, Dr. Kriegel smiles.

"Just as Tesla recognized the power of three, witches recognize the power of thirteen. Thirteen represents the Divine Feminine. There are physiologically thirteen menstrual cycles in the year. Thirteen months and thirteen menses every year. You think there's twelve months in a year?" She shakes her head. "Nope. Our current calendar is wrong. You might be surprised to find that the ancients had thirteen months. The ancient Babylonians and Hebrews added a month every few years to more perfectly align with our 365-day year. The Chinese calendar also does this. The Ancient Egyptians had thirteen months: twelve months and an extra *month* for a handful of days. In class, you remember that we learned of the power of the moon, or the goddess Diana, for worship by pagans. See, the moon aligns with Divine Feminine power.

"How about horoscopes? Only *twelve* horoscopes? Nope... notice I said thirteen signs in the zodiac. The serpent represented in the sign Ophiuchus, an unofficial sign in the zodiac, spanning late November to mid-December." A serpent in a circle pops up on the projector screen behind her. "Think you're a Sagittarius? Well, if you were born in early December, sorry to bring you bad news, but you're actually a snake." There's more laughter. "See the calendar and horoscope are all about the moon. That's the Divine Feminine. And that, my friends, is witchcraft and Mother Nature.

"Gerald Gardner's thirteen witches making up a coven brings us back to the pagan tradition celebrating thirteen moons, or months. Get it? What's more powerful than lunar magic? According to Gardner, the coven practices rites in a group with twelve women and one High Priest. The male counterpart to the Divine Feminine—the divine male—is the High Priest or serpent bearer, Ophiuchus. The snake." She points behind her at the snake in a circle eating its own tail. "The outlier *male* completes the circle forming the Divine Feminine. He is the thirteenth member. Understand? The male force counteracts the High Priestess's magic in the coven. This balance creates powerful magic. Just as Aleister Crowley believed in the power of opposites, the yin and yang, a Wiccan coven holds a similar celestial balance. For Gerald Gardner was personally influenced by Aleister Crowley as well (but that's a whole other topic).

"And that's it, guys," she says raising her arms. "That's why witches practice in groups of thirteen in covens, Dr. Kriegel."

She fumbles with the microphone on her collar. Then she hands it back to Dr. Kriegel. That brings out a thunder of applause from the crowd, and everybody goes crazy. Dr. Kriegel turns to all of us and raises his hands up high and claps too. Alondra bows, giddy, and then makes her way down the stairs and back to our seats.

"But, if I recall, Ms. Billington," Dr. Kriegel adds as Alondra makes her way down our aisle, "a group of three witches is still acceptable in a coven, according to Gardner?"

"Yes, professor," Alondra says, standing over my seat. "Well, that's part of the magic of threes I first spoke about. He believed in the power of the trinity. But the true power in a coven comes from that *unlucky* number thirteen."

"And there you have it," Dr. Kriegel says, raising his hands and clapping again. "Excellent, Ms. Billington. Excellent. The reason for thirteen in a coven. When she told me all about this at office hours, I told her she had to go over this stuff with you all in class. Her knowledge of numerology is impressive. Like I said, anybody else who wants to lecture, just ask me and we'll schedule you this semester."

And, boy, that was the wrong thing to say. Sitting beside me, Bill looks livid.

"Amazing, Allie," I say, reaching over and rubbing her back as she sits down.

"Thanks, babe."

Alondra glances at Billy. Bill ignores her, folds his arms, and glares furiously at our professor.

4

BREAKFAST AND A BEER

Bill throws open his fridge door. There's not much inside the refrigerator except beer. Yet, despite his raging, he grabs two beer bottles and opens both with a bottle opener on the counter.

I'm sitting on a couch in the living room of his apartment. It only takes a handful of steps for him to traverse the apartment from the kitchen and hand me one.

Bill's apartment is small. He lives only a mile or two from campus. There's a balcony in front of each studio apartment, motel style. And one large window opens up to that outside balcony. The apartment has two rooms—sort of. A wall partially divides his bedroom. The kitchen is part of the living room. And that's it. My friend always has the curtains drawn so, right now, though it's afternoon, a yellow-brown hue fills the place. Books and boxes are strewn everywhere on the floor. He just moved in, but he never really bothers to put things away after he takes them out. The place is a complete pig sty—but that's my friend Billy.

"Thanks," I say, taking the beer. Then I plop back down on the couch facing a TV. "Dude, chill out."

"Do you have any idea how many times I hung with Dr. Kriegel, listening to all his shit over his goddamn wife, just to find the right time to ask permission to do a lecture? Like I gave a shit about his marital problems. But I prevailed. I listened. Until one morning, he said *yes*. He said yes, Liam. *That was the same fucking goddamn morning your bitch girlfriend chose to lecture on numerology bullshit as a student!*"

I sip beer. Then I fail at holding back a chuckle.

"This is really too early for this," I say, looking at the beer bottle.

"Fuck you," he drawls. "Enjoy drinking a beer with your friend to celebrate my humiliation. Hey...maybe that's what this is all about? Some sort of satanic humiliation ritual. That witch is *such* a bitch!"

"Bill, she didn't mean to hurt your feelings."

"What are you talking about? And why don't you wipe that fucking grin off your face, Lee? I'll be the one with the last laugh over Alondra." He guzzles down beer. "I tell you what, your fucking girlfriend is going to hurt you. Remember when you were leaving her when I first came to campus? I remember. I didn't know how much poison that piece of ass really has in her fangs. If I had, as your friend, I would have dragged you the hell out of here."

"Come on. She's not that bad."

"She's plenty bad," he says, shaking his head. "She asked our professor to do that lecture just to compete with me. Just to thumb her nose at me. My lecture was good, mind you."

"Bill," I say, shaking my head. "How would she know about you lecturing that morning?"

"Open your eyes, man. Dr. Kriegel wants to work with her in Hawthorne as a grad student. I see her kissing his ass every week in office hours. All that shit about opening the class to students was just an excuse to let your leader of her cult come up on stage and prove her dominance over me. Her *Divine*

Feminine. Yeah. Well, I tell you what, I'm gonna show her some goddamn Divine Masculine."

"Okay, Bill. Look, I told you I talked to her and told her you were upset. She says she didn't mean to hurt you. I believe her. She honestly had no idea you were planning to lecture that day."

"She came to apologize to me too. First of all, I don't believe her. Like I said, she spoke with Kriegel enough to know his schedule. Second, fuck if I care now, because the damage is done."

He pulls over a kitchen chair and plops down beside me. Then he drinks more beer while running his hand through his short hair, looking miserable. He grabs a TV remote off the end table and turns on some movie with a car chase. He paid for cable. It's one of the advantages I have living with him or Alondra that I never had last year in the dorms. I mean, Alondra doesn't watch much TV. She's a witch. But she has the option to, of course, because she's rich.

"What the hell else did she say to you about me?" he asks, staring at the TV and pretending not to be interested.

"She wants to invite you to our house this week. Look, do you drink every morning and afternoon like this? It's really gross."

"Never mind." He looks over and there's a slight hint of a curl in his lips. "You mean she's finally inviting me to her place for a sabbath?"

"I don't know. Maybe. She wants you to come to dinner Friday night at her place. She's inviting both of us. I'm not sure what it all means. I don't know if she wants you in on the ritual later. She's as mysterious to me as she is to you. But she's hinted at letting you in. She knows you want in on the coven. Her pissing you off might be just what you needed. She might be letting you in after all this, man. She knows the coven is partly why you transferred to Hawthorne."

"Partly!" he snaps. *"Partly!* She knows damn well that's the

reason I came here, Lee! That bitch knows far more than she lets on. That's part of her vileness."

"Dude, chill out. She's my girlfriend."

"Sure...well...I guess if she invites me to join one of her ceremonies, then, like I said at lecture, all will be forgiven."

I shake my head and laugh. He grins for the first time. Then he raises his beer bottle in a toast. I shake my head.

"It's all you ever cared about, isn't it, Billy?"

"Yeah. Pretty much."

5

HER DOLLY

I STILL HAVE MY ARM DRAPED OVER ALONDRA AS SHE LIES ON HER side. Her soft naked breast undulates slowly under my hand as she breathes quietly in and out beneath the covers. It's soothing. Looking over her shoulder through the huge window of her bedroom, overlooking the woods, I notice it's clear outside and I can see into the forest. I think it's brighter outside than in the unlit room. The trees go for miles surrounding her dark, shadowy backyard glade. It's an amazing view but, this late with all those shadows in the surrounding forest, it's a bit spooky.

Slowly and carefully, I let go of her.

Standing in the dark naked, I crouch down and run my hands over the bedsheets, searching for my underwear. I throw my briefs on and quietly walk out of the room and head down the stairs.

By the bottom step, I nearly trip when our small black cat runs across the foyer.

"Shit, Sheba!" I snap in a forced whisper. "You scared the hell out of me!"

The cat lets out a high-pitched meow and scurries off.

I glance back upstairs. It's still dark and quiet.

Then I make my way down the hallway to my room, the guest room. Switching on the lamp by the bed, I haul up my backpack from under the bed and pull out my Addiction Medicine textbook.

Luckily, most of my studying is review. Doctor Thorbrough pretty much tells you everything in the textbook in lecture and tests off the book. I have to memorize two charts on illicit drugs, like heroin and cocaine.

As my eyes drift and I'm feeling drowsy, I startle seeing something on the dresser across from the bed: a book that shouldn't be there. It's an old leather-bound book, not a textbook, or just any book, but *the book*. Escoba's Book of Shadows, *Broomstick*. The one Lucius, Agnes, and Kenosha just wanted to "touch." The book that's like heroin or cocaine for witches.

What in the hell is it doing out in the open on my dresser? I've read it here and there over the months, on an occasional whim, but it's never just popped up on its own in my room. When I'm not reading it, I always hide it under a tree trunk in our backyard.

Did Allie find it and leave it here?

I grab the book, replacing my textbook on my lap with *Broomstick*. Then I open it.

Strangely, in a book full of writing, it opens to a blank white page—just like the blank page Lucius was conjuring up in Raleigh.

Black symbols appear. They're not handwritten, like Alondra's message, they're just appearing as if being stamped on the pages: crosses, stars, circles—the symbols intersecting each other like leaves on trees. It's as if they're being magically stamped on the white sheets. But as soon as they appear, they disappear.

One distinctive symbol appears in the center. It's a black checkered figure with stars between two lines in the center. It flashes over and over, in the center, like a broken billboard sign. And every time it appears, I feel pain in my forehead.

There's children's laughter. The laughter sounds like it comes from outside the window, as if kids are playing outside —which is impossible because it's the middle of the night.

Then I shudder. I recognize the voices. Not the words, the kids' thick southern accents. My heart races. My body stiffens. It's the two sisters that appeared on campus when I was possessed last year, the girls from that terrifying freak-house in Geneva Forest in Alabama. Their voices haunted me last year when I was possessed.

"Walpurgisnacht. Walpurgisnacht. Walpurgisnacht."

The words seem to be announced by a hundred voices inside the walls.

The lamp light goes out and I'm left in darkness.

The door creaks open.

Jumping up to switch the light on, I lurch back. A little girl's under me in the shadows by the threshold. It's one of the girls from that house in Geneva Forest, now lankier. I can't tell if it's Melanie or her older sister, Winona. The sisters always looked similar in their short white dresses. In the past, the girl was in pigtails, but now her dark hair is long and disheveled.

"What's that in your hands?" she asks quietly. "Does that book belong to you? Or does it belong to the lady upstairs?" She giggles. "I like magical books. My sister Winnie and I, we used to have so much fun with them. We'd play with sticks and stars and cards. Ever play with sticks, stars, and cards? I have a whole deck. You like that book? I see you reading it a lot. Do you want to play with me and my sister right now using your book?"

"Is that you, Melanie?"

Her face in the shadows looks like Melanie.

A lady's voice screams. *That sounds like Alondra!* I whirl around, but all I see is the draped window behind me.

When I turn back, Melanie's gone.

"Do you... wanna...play with my dolly?" Melanie's voice asks in the outside hallway. "Hmm?" She sounds like she's dragging something. She returns in the doorway. "She's...she's a bit heavy. Might need your big strong arms to help me move her into your room."

She drags into my room an unconscious girl with a matching white dress. It's as if she's holding a dead doll. But I recognize the face in her arms. It's Winona.

"Come Lammas, witches love playing with dollies," Melanie says, stopping in the doorway. "Do you wanna play with my dolly? We used to have so much fun playing games together, my sister and I." She stops and stares down at her sister. "Why, I remember a doll I hid under the dirt. Buried it with Momma's bottle. Got so tired of Momma and Winnie crying and crying all the time, asking me where I hid it. Momma used to use the bottle to stop all her crying. Well, one day I got so fed up with Momma's crying that, well, I decided to hide her bottle. I hid it with a doll to make sure she'd never find it." Melanie laughs. "You should have seen my momma." Then she gazes at me. I lurch back. Her eyes have turned a glowing pearly white. "Winnie came right out into our yard and went digging all over the place, so worried about my poor mommy and her sickness." Melanie bends over, laughing. "It was so funny. So funny. I couldn't stop laughing. But the strange thing is...you know, the strange thing is...Momma never found her bottle. That bottle was full of all sorts of magic things to help her smile. But the strange thing is, she never, ever found it. But I found my dolly, Mr. Johansen. I sure did. And then Momma kept hollering at me, not able to sleep that night. Isn't that funny?"

Melanie looks up with a devilish grin, her eyes still glowing white. But then her whole body shakes as if she's afraid. Or is she laughing?

"What's going on!"

"Don't you remember? Don't you recall what me and my sister used to say? You're a pussy-sucking cunt, Liam. And you're going straight to Sheol. You remember how it all goes, don't you? Let's see—" She looks up and then grows a sly grin, drawling. "F-uck-ed... F-uck-ed. That's it. You can say it with me. *Fucked* by a witch, six—"

"*What's happening!*"

"*Walpurgisnacht! Walpurgisnacht! Walpurgisnacht!*"

This foreign word is shouted, as if by a hundred voices in the room. But then Melanie and her sister vanish.

The door's still ajar. I quake just wondering what's in the corner in the darkness.

The whole house starts shaking. It's as if there's an earthquake and the entire house is quaking in fear, just like Melanie was.

Is this a nightmare? Am I dreaming this? It's as if that haunted house in Geneva Forest is my house now.

Melanie appears again by the door. Her white eyes glow and she grins, holding her sister again.

"Pray tell, warlock? Pray tell. Six, six, six. Fucked by a witch. Six, six, six. Fucked by a witch. Is the nasty one upstairs? Is she? Remember what Alondra said to me and my sister, Liam? I remember. *Let's fuck in front of the children*, she said. *Come on, Lee. Aren't I your girlfriend?*"

"*How are you even here!*"

"Pray tell," Melanie says, putting a finger to her lips, chuckling. "Pray tell. Do you know what six plus six plus six is?"

"Eighteen," says Winona, opening white eyes.

"Why, it sure is, Winnie," Melanie says, looking down at her sister in her arms. "It sure is. And what's one plus eight, sister?"

"*Nein! Nein! Nein!*"

The light switches back on. But that's no less terrifying with the girl and her dead sister still at the threshold of my room.

"*Walpurgisnacht!*" Melanie barks up at me. "*Walpurgisnacht! Walpurgisnacht! Verbrenne die hexe! Wer glaubt und sich taufen lässt, wird gerettet; und wer nicht glaubt, wird verurteilt warden! Verbrenne die hexe! Verbrenne die hexe!*"

"*Lee! Come here! Come here, quick!*" That's Alondra shouting upstairs this time. She sounds hurt!

I don't care about the freak anymore. I throw the book on the ground and rush past Melanie into the dark hallway and then quickly make my way upstairs.

There's a sound of tearing along the walls. And children's laughter trails behind me.

I barge into the bedroom.

Red. All I see is red. It's like a red glow comes from the ceiling. All shines crimson. And the white bedsheets are soaking wet. The body replacing my girlfriend is no longer human. It's more like a large carcass, a mound of bloody flesh emitting a horrible rotting-meat smell, as if roadkill has been thrown onto her bed.

"*Lee!*" Allie cries. "*Lee! My god! Come here!*" Alondra's panicked voice is coming from outside the hall. "*Quick!*"

Glancing outside through the large bedroom window, I see a fire raging below in our backyard glade. It's a central bonfire, larger than normal. And circling the fire is a group of women in red robes.

"*Walpurgisnacht! Walpurgisnacht! Walpurgisnacht!*"

"*Liam!*"

I rush down the hallway, nearly colliding with a wall.

In our small study, Alondra's in her black nightgown crazily rummaging through desk drawers. A red glow still shines behind me, but the red slowly turns yellow from the lamplight in the small room.

The room contains only a chaise lounge and her bookcase, but she has boxes stacked all over the floor. Allie's in full panic mode, searching all the books on the bookcase in her study and then throwing them off the shelves. She drops to the ground and starts rummaging through the boxes, tossing jars, candles, and books to the side. And then she returns to rummaging through books on the bookcase.

"What the hell's going on?"

"Where is it!" Alondra asks. "Damn it. Did you feel that, Lee? There's a presence invading the house."

Uh, yeah, I felt it. I saw it.

She stands up, looking everywhere around the room. But then she's at it again, searching more shelves and throwing a cordless phone and more books off another shelf.

"We have to find it."

"What are you looking for?"

"The source."

She grabs a small crystal ball on the shelf and peers into it for a second. This ball is cracked. I've seen her sit on the only furniture in the room, the chaise lounge, just staring into this glass orb on her lap. She shakes her head, lays it down on the floor, and moves on to opening another box. She moves a box of small glass vials full of dirt, staring at them.

It's then that I realize the main light is switched off, so I go to switch it on.

"Keep the lights off!"

"Yeah, I felt it, Allie. I sure did. Actually, I saw it."

"What?" She stops and finally turns to me. "What do you mean, you saw it? What did you see, Lee?"

"Melanie came into my room downstairs."

"Who?" She stands up and touches my arm. Then she searches my eyes. "Lee, this is vital. What happened downstairs?"

"I was studying a book."

"What book!"

I hesitate. For months, I've kept mum about taking *Broomstick* from its hiding place and reading it. It's like a portal into my dreams. Awake dreams. And opening and reading it sometimes makes me feel good. But I've never dared tell her. And never has it appeared by itself in the room before.

Alondra looks down and shakes her head. "This house is my hallowed ground. It takes a very powerful spirit to invade it."

"*Broomstick.*"

"*Broomstick?*" Alondra asks, looking up. "Yes, *Broomstick.* I'd believe that. That would be powerful enough. Lee...were you... *Fuck! Were you casting from my book?*" Her eyes open wide. *"Are you actually casting magic from my book, Liam!"*

"Of course not! How would I even know how—"

But she drops to the ground and grabs the book from the carpet. *Broomstick* was lying right by my feet. *What?!* I remember throwing the grimoire on the floor downstairs.

"Switch the light on," she demands. "Quick. Turn it on. I need to figure out what you were reading."

"I thought you wanted the light off?"

"Lee, this isn't a time to teach you things. Stop fucking asking me questions and turn on the goddamn light."

I switch the light on.

Everything appears normal. Too normal. I think that's even more unsettling. Allie's just sitting cross-legged on the carpet with *Broomstick* on her lap flipping through pages. But that's when the *normal* stops. As she raises her palm over the book, like Lucius did, the pages turn by themselves.

I hear something fall downstairs. I turn to the hallway and have the terrifying thought that Melanie could appear behind me dragging her dead sister again. All I see behind me are dark shadows in the hallway.

When I turn back, Allie's staring up at me from the book. She doesn't seem to be frantic anymore. She looks pissed.

"*I can't use the book but you fucking can! Is that how this works, Liam?* How long have you been casting from my grimoire? Tell me the truth. Do you have any idea how dangerous it is to cast spells from this book without any knowledge of magic?"

"I...I haven't. What are you talking about? I haven't been casting. I...anyway, it's my book, Alondra...but, look, I don't even know how to cast magic."

"You took my book, Lee. The book thinks you're the owner. You open it, glance at it—god help you—read it, or do whatever the fuck you do with it, and it can take possession of you. Particularly you, who isn't even a witch." She stands up and heaves a sigh, running her hand through her long hair. "Shit." She shakes her head. "Shit. I'm sorry…just, this is so dangerous. How many times have you opened my Book of Shadows and read from it?"

Over the past few months, maybe twenty times. But I'm not going to tell her that.

"Once or twice."

"Lee, there's a spirit haunting this house. You need to be honest with me."

"No shit, Allie. I saw the sisters again. Melanie was dragging her dead sister into the guest room."

"Who?"

"Melanie. That little girl in Geneva Forest. Winona's sister. The girls in that house that possessed me."

"Kenosha and Agnes got rid of your possession," she says, shaking her head. "And the girls aren't possessed either, after our ritual."

"Well, Allie, I saw Melanie downstairs in my room. She was dragging her sister about like a dead doll. She kept asking me if I wanted to play with *her*—her dead sister. It was very sick and very real. Then, when I came up to the bedroom, you were gone. Our bedroom just had some dead animal on the bed and was red. And, outside by a bonfire, I saw—"

"Could those girls be casting?" Allie asks herself, turning from me. She shakes her head in disbelief. "Or is it Lucius?"

"*Vade retro, daemon!*" Alondra shouts at the book. I jump at the sudden outburst. "*Vade retro! Leave! Leave this place! This is my hallowed ground! I am the Hawthorne Witch.*"

The whole house answers by shaking again. Then we hear laughter from the two sisters coming from downstairs.

"*Oungan!*" yells Melanie downstairs. "*Oungan! Come play with us! Come and use your book of stars! Come help us!*"

Then she bursts into laughter.

Alondra slams shut the book.

There's a scream. Allie's voice screams, "*Lee! Oh my god, not you!*" But Alondra's lips are closed.

"What the hell?" asks Alondra, looking around us.

"*Vade retro*," Alondra shouts, gazing up at the ceiling in a panic. "*Vade retro. Daemonium relinquo!*" She grabs the book and holds it aloft with two shaky hands, aiming it at the walls and ceiling in different directions. "I call upon the power of Escoba Hawthorne. Be gone from my house! How dare you be present here! I am the Hawthorne Witch and this is my hallowed ground! I call on the power of Escoba's Book of Shadows and Grimoire to demand that you leave this place! Leave this hallowed ground, demons, now!"

"Abaddon witch," says another woman's voice. This voice sounds like Kenosha's. "Hawthorne will never be your hallowed ground."

"Come help us, Liam," Melanie shouts downstairs. She's not sounding derisive—she sounds desperate. "Please. Come help Momma and Pa with your book. Please! You just have to. Come to our house with the book and help us! Momma and Pa are really sick."

But then...complete silence.

"Lee," Alondra says, wagging the book at me, "don't ever open this book again, a'ight? Never. Don't open it. You don't want me to have it? Fine. Hide it. But don't you dare open and cast from it ever again. 'kay? Fuck." She runs her hands through her long hair, shaking her head. "Promise. Promise me, Lee. Don't ever open this book again. Never. Promise."

"Sure thing, Alondra. But how can I be casting? I'm not even a witch."

"The book thinks you are."

"Allie, I didn't cast any magic. The book appeared and then opened by itself. Then Melanie appeared."

She heaves a sigh. "Okay," she says. "Fine."

"Is Melanie gone?"

"Babe, there's no way a little girl can haunt this house. This is the hallowed ground of the Hawthorne coven. I'd believe Escoba's ghost was haunting us before I'd believe that."

"Then who? Kenosha?"

"Maybe. You have to tell me anything that happens around that book, okay? You see a vision, tell me. I have a lot of dangerous stuff in my house, particularly in this room. Don't ever touch anything in this room. And don't open that book again. Promise. Hide it, fine. But don't open it again."

"I won't be opening it now," I say with a sigh. And I walk over to the chaise lounge and plop down. Then I put my head in my hands. "Sorry."

"Sweet," she says. And she actually chuckles. "How would you know?"

"How do you know a spirit is using the book?"

"That book isn't a presence, it's a tool. The book isn't dangerous, it's only as dangerous as whoever uses it. Someone, or some presence, is tempting you with its power. Channeling through you. The book opened to a page flashing the sigil Ogou. In Africa, Ogun is the war god. It's a masculine symbol. The hunter god. In Haitian Vodou, it represents the male leader. Their Ouroboros. Apparently, someone's calling out for you to cast spells as an Oungan."

"What's an Oungan?"

"A High Priest. In voodoo, a male voodoo priest. That book is a voodoo grimoire of Escoba's, remember? You're representing the divine male force in Hawthorne because of our lack of one." She runs her hands through her long hair. "Look, Lee, it was not only a dick move to take advantage of my protection that night with my onyx stone and then steal my book—" She puts her hand up. "It was. But it was also stupid. When we made up, I came to check on you. Not only because I love you, but because I was worried. Your usual hot-headedness led you to do something really dangerous. That book is one of the most powerful talismans there ever was, and you took possession of it. Along with Marie Laveau, Moll Dyer, Alice Kyteler, Escoba is one of the most powerful witches there ever was. So was her grimoire. And you stupidly took ownership of it. Somebody is scrying and conjuring magic through the book to reach you."

"Melanie."

"A little girl can't scry on my hallowed ground. And she just cried out for help. Maybe Kenosha's messing with her house again?"

"What about Lucius?"

"Maybe. But why would he attack? I'm offering him everything his order wants if he joins the coven. It's probably Kenosha and her damn Crescent coven again."

"The demon impersonating her sure looked like Melanie, Allie. She was older, but the same girl. Her voice and her appearance were vivid. It felt like Melanie was really in our house."

"I felt a powerful demonic presence here," she says with a nod. "I felt it in the walls. Someone is casting goetia."

"But now...it's gone. Right, Allie?"

"Sure."

6

——————

THIRTEEN

BILL AND I KNOCK ON THE FRONT DOOR OF ALONDRA'S HOUSE. And that feels weird. Because it's also my house. But it's Friday night, and Friday is the only time Allie doesn't allow me to just drop in, because it's sabbath ritual night for her witches. Behind me, in the driveway, in front of and behind Alondra's elegant red nineteenth-century carriage, are parked a bunch of cars belonging to all the girls in her coven.

"Hey, Lee," says Rachel, bubbly as always, with a big smile as she throws open the door. She gives me a hug. "God, we missed you so much!" Then she glances at Bill. "Hey, stranger."

Rachel's dressed in one of our black Druid-like cloaks. Her golden blond hair seems yellower than usual. Thick black goth makeup covers her eyelids and lips, and she is wearing her black robe. And she has a half moon drawn on her forehead.

"Hey, Rachel," Bill says.

"You guys hungry?" asks Rachel. "Holly brought in food and everyone's eating. But we were waiting for you before starting the meeting."

I smell roasted chicken. Sheba creeps in from the adjacent living room. I lift her into my arms, petting her. Meanwhile, the dining room apparently has every witch from Allie's coven because, as we're making our way down the hall, all the raucousness seems to be coming from there.

When we turn left into the room, it looks strange. Sitting around Alondra's large, regal mahogany dining table are all her friends in black cloaks. It's as if friars in a monastery got together for supper in a church in medieval England. But with hoods off, and all that long hair and dark gothic makeup, it's just witches chatting and dining. Still, all that weirdness is nothing compared to Allie's third guest. Sitting next to Allie, with his back to the large window, is a bald man with a goatee wearing another black robe with a red satin interior: *the doctor.* Two seats are available, facing our huge window looking out on the forest. These two seats are obviously meant for Bill and me. So we sit across from Satan. Amusingly, Bill and Lucius look at each other with smiles. I think Bill is fascinated by this devil.

"Hey, Liam," says Alondra with a grin. "Bill. Come join us. We're holding a special meeting before heading outdoors for ceremony. Grab a glass of wine and enjoy yourselves."

Holly, about a head shorter than Rachel, comes by and puts two slices of chicken on Bill's and my plates. Then Beth places rolls, veggies, and potatoes on the side.

"We can serve ourselves," I say with a chuckle.

"Not tonight," says Alondra, turning oddly serious. "Tonight every man is a special guest of honor."

"Graced by the serpent Ouroboros," says Lucius across from me with a nod. The freak is acting overly confident as if I'm a guest in *his* house. "Blessed be the serpent bearer and giver of light. Hail Satan."

Then he raises his wine glass in a toast.

"To the serpent bearer," echoes Alondra, raising her glass too. Then all the girls raise their glasses of red wine and repeat "to the serpent bearer."

"But Lee's not twenty-one yet, High Priestess," teases our dark-skinned youngest recruit, Cindy, at the other end of the table. We all laugh because Cindy is barely eighteen.

"Age didn't stop you from toking out the other day, girl," replies Beth, her much older good friend. "You best shut your mouth."

"Pot isn't wine," Cindy says, sticking her tongue out at Beth.

"What's the invite all about?" I ask, sipping wine.

"Nice to be finally invited," Bill quips.

"Tonight is about men," says Alondra. She gestures to our plates. "Eat. Enjoy. We're all so happy to serve dinner for you tonight."

Then she cuts and forks chicken. And all her witches nod at us and take a bite. And then it turns really weird because everyone, in their black witch robes and makeup, just eats.

I gaze through the large window across from me at the forest. But then I shudder. Because that goatee-devil-freak is staring at me.

"I think we're ready to start, Lucius," Alondra says to him with her mouth full.

"I'm honored for the opportunity to speak to your coven, Falconsong," Lucius says. "The arrangement between my coven and yours will be temporary, of course. But the hope is that we may enter into a long-standing agreement. Just as the cosmic wheel turns, as Ouroboros chases its tail the snake does not consume the tail, but perpetually chases itself. This is and this shall be. As above, so below. From the base of the tree of life, to the top, and then returning back down again. Over and over in harmony. One energy to another. Now proposed by your esteemed leader to seal this agreement, a patch to close this gap formed by the departure of your former High Priest. That is, if you permit my ascension."

Alondra nods. But then she returns to cutting chicken with a fork and knife and eating.

I don't know what the fuck he's talking about.

"Here is my proposal," he continues. "My sisters and brothers in my order are not interested in residing here in Hawthorne. My order is based too far from here. And so, I propose we meet metaphysically. Astrally. We may channel our powers upon the forces of the flame through divination. Your bonfire can be used to scry with my order, and no one will ever need to be present. On the occasion of our holiest Sabbaths, we can meet. But my circle agrees to come to Hawthorne only upon our holiest of holidays. But outside of those events, if permitted, we may continue to communicate by the power of the pentagram.

"And so, I preside over your vote. It's up to each one of you if you wish to proceed. Just because your High Priestess desires it, does not mean that you do. You all must decide for yourself. But Falconsong has told me that she desires that the decision is made unanimously by each one of you here in this circle."

"Allie," says Rachel. "Can we speak freely before the uninitiated?" At first, I'm thinking she's referring to Lucius, but Rachel points at me and Bill.

"That's why they were invited, White Dove."

"Doesn't our High Priest have to be *physically* present before the fire for our magic to properly manifest?"

"Usually, yes," Alondra says, drinking more wine thoughtfully. "But Lucius suggests our power is enough that he believes we can scry and accomplish the same thing."

"What about sacrifice?" asks Beth. "Or..." Beth looks uneasily over at Bill and me. "Consecrated union?"

"I assure you, everything needed can be accomplished by divination," replies Lucius. As he strokes the stem of his crystal wine glass, he creeps me out more when I notice his rather long nails. At least he doesn't have his snake slithering on his neck tonight. "That is, if the uninitiated permits it."

And then he oddly looks at me.

"What?"

Alondra turns to me too. She looks nervous, and for Allie to look worried over anything makes me even more worried.

"Liam, we need your permission," Alondra says. "We think

that the only way for this arrangement to work is for you to let me use your book."

"*Your book*, Falconsong," corrects Lucius. Then he leans forward, steepling his hands as if challenging me. "*Broomstick* belongs to the High Priestess of the Hawthorne coven. It is your coven's grimoire. In order to scry from such a distance *and* perform ritualistic magic, we need a very powerful talisman. We believe the grimoire of the Hawthorne coven can make it work. We need to use *Broomstick*."

"I can't do that," I say, shaking my head. "I swore to Kenosha and Agnes that I'd never part with it. I swore that I'd keep it from you, Allie."

"I know you did," Alondra says slowly and carefully. "But, Liam, if the group accepts this new arrangement, *if*...it will be the only way for Lucius and his circle to work with us. We could relocate, but then we wouldn't be the Hawthorne coven, would we? And we wouldn't be attending college. A compromise is needed. So...Rachel's right, magic will not be at its full potential with any everyday black mirror. Any sort of mirror or crystal ball won't do. We need a powerful talisman. Only by the power of Escoba Hawthorne's grimoire can we convene rituals apart from one another over so great a distance.

"I think all my sisters at this table will accept Lucius into our coven tonight. We can continue to practice our magic in the way we're supposed to. As witches. We're witches, Lee, and we need to do what we do. You get that. But...the only way for this to work in ritual on our Sabbaths is by using your book."

I shake my head again.

"Liam," Alondra adds, raising her brow, "when you think about it, I'm not violating your wishes or that of the witch council. If you agree, it will be only with your consent. It will remain your book, and you can take it back at any time." And she turns to Lucius. "But Lucius, you're wrong. The book belongs to Liam. The decision is his alone. I respect that." Lucius glares at me. Then Alondra sighs and adds, "I only need to use your book on our blessed sabbath once a week, babe. You can go back to hiding it after. It will be used only for the purpose of communication between our groups. I'll swear to that. That will be it."

"Your High Priestess proposes only a temporary arrangement for a few moons," Lucius says. "For now, I can do this favor with my order to continue to preserve your coven until you work on another replacement. It will not be for much more than a year, at the most."

And then he glances at Bill. Bill nods.

"The vote is tonight, sisters," Alondra says, addressing the rest of the table. "Will you work with Lucius, or will we continue to be without the full power of Hecate?"

"I think you know our decision already, High Priestess," Rachel says. And many other witches around the table nod.

"Alondra, the man across from me is as close as you'll ever get to inviting the devil into your coven," I say. "How could you consider bringing him in? He's an admitted Satanist—"

"That's not your business," Alondra snaps, shaking her head. "You're not voting on whether Lucius will join us. You're here to decide whether you will let us use your book."

"I said no."

"I need your book to cast witchcraft, Liam," Alondra snaps. "You know what happened to us the other night. It's getting dangerous here. We have to investigate who attacked my hallowed ground. There are many forces out there like the group who murdered my parents. Your book and our casting can help reveal our enemies."

"Jane told me that your parents were killed by a madman."

"It was a coven. Now, with their order, I might be able to investigate—"

"Are you going to go sell your soul to the devil in order to find out?"

"*Sure!*" she snaps. "But that's none of your fucking business either, Lee." But then she closes her eyes and takes a deep breath. I look around the room, and all the other witches are staring at us. Allie throws her long hair back and mutters. "My soul isn't your business either." Then she sighs. "Look, it's not right to invite you to our meeting and fight. Everyone here knows I love you to death, but your book is vitally important." She raises her palm. "My parents' death isn't your business. Whether Lucius joins is not your business. This isn't why you were invited tonight. I invited you to ask to use your book."

"You're right," I say, sighing and running my fingers through my thin hair, "it's hardly appropriate to talk about personal—"

"That is where you are in error, sir," says Lucius, raising a finger. "Your High Priestess apologized for embarrassing you, not for talking publicly in front of her friends. You think of privacy only because you are not a practicing warlock in a coven. You do not understand. Every sister before you is intertwined with the woman you love. There is no privacy with a High Priestess and her coven. That is why it is called a coven. That is the unity of the higher self, visualized by the High Priestess tarot card upon the precipice of D'at. That is the unity of Hecate magi."

"Why do you talk like a professor?" I ask.

"Lucius studied magic at Cambridge," Alondra answers dismissively. "He came to the States and taught as a professor at Emory."

That hardly calms me. It only angers me more. It's so typical of Alondra to throw a zinger at me that's designed to confuse, or impress, me. It's like Dr. Kriedel's zingers in lecture, only Allie lives with these zingers all the time in her real life. It's this mystery that I both love and loathe.

Of course, Lucius's lips just curl in a vile satanic, sardonic smirk.

"Excuse me, *doctor*," I reply, "but I thought you referred to me as a warlock in Raleigh?"

"You are a warlock. I said you are not a *practicing* warlock. Your education is lacking. You are ignorant in magic, sir. A coven has strength through the group's unity in ritual. Everyone here, except you and your friend, have been initiated to be one single unit. That is the power of a female's coven. That is why it is called a coven. You are a warlock, of course, but you have not been recognized or taught magic in ceremony. My group is different." He pauses from lecturing me to sip some wine. Then he turns to the others. "Our order emphasizes individualism and is, therefore, more in tune with our independent desires. Our will. Magic may manifest in that way as well. Our group's power comes by the gnosis of the power within, much of it by the avatar and ego. God exists in all of us, yes? As above, so below. As said in your Christian Bible: *regnum dei intra vos est*. That is the difference between my order and your coven.

"You witches are just as powerful, simply casting your energies in a different way...in a more, dare I say, democratic way."

Then the son of a bitch pats his lips with his white cloth napkin.

"If you allow me to work with you witches, I can teach you these things. It is, of course, a hardship for me and my group to congregate in your forest town. But as a favor for Alondra, out of my deep and profound respect for your leader's power, we can create this agreement, sealed in blood, that will help get you through this difficult time together."

"All based on whether I let you use my book," I remark.

"Yes," replies Lucius. "Indeed." Then he laughs. "But I've already foreseen you will. Resist in words, Liam, but I know your heart, warlock. I know very well that you will use the book again. And my respect for Alondra extends to my future respect for you. I am aware that I cannot move forward without your acquiescence. But I also know that you do not see your love and respect for everyone at this table. When you see what all you and your friends are, and that you are already a part of it, you'll agree to help. Then, perhaps then, Liam, you will no longer need me. For then, you will be the practicing warlock you were meant to be."

And he raises his wine glass, as if in a toast. Then he goes back to cutting some chicken, staring down at his plate, and ignoring everyone staring at him, because the pompous ass is, apparently, finished talking.

"Well, you'll have to come to Hawthorne with your circle, Lucius," I say. "I already swore to other witches that I won't let Alondra—"

"Enough, Liam," Alondra interjects. "Don't fight."

Me? I'm fighting...

"Your High Priestess warned me about your rigidity," Lucius says with a chuckle, chewing on chicken. "I think if you weren't so stubborn, the solution would be simple. Then all of this tension would be over, and the Hawthorne coven would be whole. You wouldn't have to give the book to anyone. You simply would use it yourself."

"The answer's no." I turn to Alondra. "No, Alondra, I will never lend my book for ceremonies. You keep telling me how dangerous it is. Why should any witch be using it? Sorry, but I promised Kenosha and Agnes I'd guard the book."

Lucius shrugs and just returns to eating.

But everyone else turns very quiet. Many have their heads down. I think, in the silence, they all hate me. A few, even my good friend Rachel, look really pissed.

"I'll talk with him," Alondra says dismissively. "Liam's decision does not have to be made tonight." Then she turns to me. "After we eat, Lee, I ask that you be excused from tonight's meeting. Please understand our coven's privacy tonight when we vote for our High Priest."

Lucius annoyingly nods between swallows and more cuts of his chicken between his fork and knife.

"Bill, I ask that you remain with us during ceremony outside by the bonfire," Alondra adds. "Do you want to participate with us tonight?"

Well, at least someone looks happy at the dinner table now.

~

"*Why did you even invite me!*"

We're alone in the house, cleaning all the dishes off the dining room table. Everyone's gone except Sheba, who scurries off after hearing my raging. The rest of the night, during their ritual, I was back in my room studying. But when it was late enough, and I was sure all her friends were gone—along with her infernal devil-guest—I ran into the dining room to finally let out my fury.

"I really don't want to fight, Liam," Allie says with a sigh, grabbing some wine glasses and a porcelain plate. I grab a few glasses and follow her into the kitchen.

"I don't know why everything has to be such a goddamn mystery with you," I cry. "If you're gonna pull off shit like this, why keep surprising me? You want me to show someone my book for his hell house, tell me why. And tell me *before* it's in front of all our friends. Stop doing everything so secretively."

She opens the dishwasher and nods, laying some glasses on a tray. Then she heads back to the hallway with her back to me.

"I'm a witch," she says, in the dining room again. "I told you this a thousand times. You're asking me again to not be me, babe."

"Allie, he might have been right about your lack of privacy with the other witches. Maybe all your friends know your stuff, but using social influence to force my decision in front of your group was a nasty thing to do."

"Social influence?" she asks, finally stopping in the middle of the hallway. She chuckles. "That's interesting. I wouldn't know, psychologist. Maybe I acted due to my unconscious, as Freud would say." She's putting more dirty plates in the dishwasher in the kitchen. "My deep unconscious mind, a'ight? Or Jungian shadow work? Yeah, maybe Lucius represents my dark shadow that I have to finally face in the development of my atman. But you are my total white light, babe. That's for sure.

My total *lux*." She flashes a sarcastic grin. Then she heads right back to the dining room again. "You tell me, psychologist. Or just maybe, Liam, just maybe, I was inviting you to dinner to join me and my friends."

"You invited me to get the book. Next time you do something like that, I'm holding you to explaining everything. You've made it very clear before that you don't want me at our house on Friday nights."

"I don't think you want me to explain anything," she says, with a chuckle and smug grin. She snatches a handful of silverware from the dining room table. "Part of you loves my mystery." And she chuckles again. "And anyway..." We're back in the dark hallway. "We don't have to fight. Like I told the coven, the decision about your book doesn't have to be made tonight."

"I'm never giving you my book."

And I snatch her wrist. She stops and stares at my hand.

I let go.

"All right, Liam," she says with a slow nod. "Fine. I get it."

"Why'd you invite me? For the book—I get that. Okay. Fine. But...why invite my friend Bill? Why invite him of all people?"

"I wanted him to meet Lucius. I wanted his opinion regarding whether we should work with him."

"I already told you my feelings about Lucius."

"Yes, you did. Bill didn't."

"Since when do you care about Bill's opinion on anything?"

"He might not have the book, but he doesn't despise witchcraft, like you. He loves magic more than anyone I know, aside from Lucius and the witches in the council. I plan to initiate your friend." She falls back against the wall, folding her arms. "Oh, Lee, my coven needs a High Priest. That's all. You saw what's happening in our house without one. There's no mystery."

"What about Bill? Did you lecture that day to make a fool out of him?"

"What? What are you talking about? My lecture? Why the hell would I lecture to hurt your friend? We've been through this. Dr. Kriegel invited me to speak, a'ight? How was I ever going to refuse him? You know my dream is to teach in Hawthorne one day."

"Bill was supposed to teach that morning."

"And I told you already. I didn't know that."

"It seems you're always fighting with him."

"Your best friend is a fucked-up guy, okay? He came here to study witchcraft, sure. That and naked tits and ass. That's *all* he loves in his miserable, boring life, Liam. He only loves magic, the paranormal, and sex."

"Well, that sounds familiar."

"Why are we fighting! I'm not asking you to fill that position or to be initiated, a'ight? Lucius is right. You'd be the obvious choice. The coven needs a male. Okay? Thirteen. Remember my lecture? Thirteen. Until we fill that void, our circle is in trouble. You saw what happened with your book in our house. You have to understand twelve, without a male member, isn't going to cut it for protecting Hawthorne. A'ight? I need a full coven to do what I do. It's not only to conjure magic, it's for protection from the spells already cast."

"Wait. Is that why you're initiating Bill? If Lucius doesn't work out, you want to choose him to be your High Priest?"

"Why the fuck do you care?" But then she runs her hand through her long hair and shakes her head. "Actually, babe… you want to know the truth? I want *you* to be our High Priest, okay? But since you're refusing, I have to choose anyone available after Lucius leaves. Like he said, he's temporary."

"But I won't give you the book."

"Stop fucking repeating yourself, a'ight! I got it, Lee. You're not gonna let me borrow my book. Fine. I heard you a thousand times already. You don't have to keep saying that over and over! So stop fucking saying it! You won't give me the book. Fine! I heard enough already."

I look down.

But then I feel her hand gently touch my cheek.

"Oh, baby," she says very quietly. "Baby, baby, please... Please stop doing this. Please. I don't want to do this with you. I have to lead my friends. That's all. I love you so much, Liam, but...I also love my sisters. We all love the craft."

"I know."

"I don't think you do."

I nod, looking up—but then I avert my eyes.

"Oh, Liam," she says, putting her arms around me. "Try to understand." She leans her head on my shoulder. "We need to make the coven whole more than ever now. Our home was attacked."

"We'll figure it out."

7

———

GOOFER DUST

I PARK MY RED CAMARO OFF THE SIDE OF AN EMPTY ROAD. WE'RE near the woods, shadowed by trees, and it's super dark without any streetlamps along the one-lane road. These trees are not Hawthorne Forest. We're in a forest in Alabama.

To my left a dirt road meanders about a quarter mile to a barn. Bright yellow illuminates a white fence in front of a two-story wood structure out there. Bales are collected on flatter land close to the barn. It's dark, but I'm guessing it's a field for farming or for raising animals. Farming in the forest? I really don't know. I never grew up on a farm, like Alondra. On the opposite side a grassy hillside blocks my view of a sloping incline behind a long barbed-wire fence.

I open the door for her.

Alondra's in the passenger seat with her head dipped down, focusing on a small violet notebook old enough to have been written a hundred years ago. She's got many books like this in her study. *Broomstick* isn't her only ancient grimoire. There are stars and a waxing moon on the cover of this one. It's like she's studying the book—which isn't unusual either.

"So?" I ask with my hand out for her. "Mind telling me why we came all the way over here tonight?"

"It's a surprise." Then she yawns and stretches out her arms, tearing her eyes from the book. She reaches out and I help her out of my car. "Did you bring it?"

"Maybe. What did I say in our fight about secrets, Allie? I won't tell until you tell me why we had to drive three hours into another state in the middle of the night."

"Well, something has to be done after that devilish night at our house. Our peace and quiet will last only for so long. Sure, I cast a few shield spells with the coven last ceremony, but anything that had the power to attack us upon my hallowed ground won't stop with a few shield spells. You said you saw Melanie in the house? Well, I figured we'd head close to the source. It's not that I think it was actually her, but, since you saw her, I want to work with the energies here."

"It's Lucius, Allie. The timing is too coincidental."

"I haven't seen a sign of it. I know you don't like him, but he seems completely on our side. Whoever it is, I think the grounds here will help us figure it out."

"Why the middle of the night?"

"Less light means more secretive." And she smiles wide. "I'm all about that mystery you love and hate. You know why, Liam? Hmm? Do you?... I'm fun." Then she laughs and winks at me. "Come on. This is totally occult stuff. It'll be a blast. Just get my bag from the trunk and the book, wherever you're hiding it —can't wait to find out where—and we'll get this debacle over with, head back home, and curl up on the couch with some popcorn and watch a movie."

"You swear you'll give back the book after you cast your spell? I'm only lending it tonight because of what happened."

"I tell you what. If I don't return the book to you after our little venture tonight, you and I are through." And she raises a palm as if swearing an oath. "No joke. You and I are through, Liam, if I don't return the book to you. How 'bout that? And you know how much I'm madly in love with you, babe. So, stop. Just go to the trunk, get the duffel bag, and get the book."

"But...wait," she says, snatching my elbow. "First a kiss, handsome. You were so cute, Lee, with Dad last night."

"I'm not sure he likes me."

"He absolutely adored you, Lee. Just like I do."

She laughs again as she kisses my lips. Then she pulls me closer, and we smooch by the car door. And as I help her out of the car, I'm still touching her lips.

She finally disengages and reaches back into the car to grab my heavy navy-blue coat from the back seat and her black leather jacket to go with her black blouse and jeans. I take out of the trunk the very large duffel bag Alondra brought. It has a small lock on the zipper, for some reason.

"Is there a dead body inside this bag?"

"Could be," she says with a laugh.

"And you're not going to tell me?"

"Nope."

"Mind at least telling me why you're in such a good mood?"

"I told you. This is exciting. We're going to practice witch-craft together. That's even better than ghost hunting. I wish we could do it all the time. Now come on. Where'd you hide my book? Or...I mean *your* book. I'm dying to know."

"You promise you'll hand it back to me?"

"I told you already." She lifts up her palm again. "If I don't, it's finally over between us."

"You really think your dad liked me?"

"Oh, stop it. He did. But that's not hard. Uncle Hanley loves everybody."

"I didn't like how you guys were teasing me."

"We thought you were so cute. Especially over your problems opening the wine bottle. That was hilarious. He loves you, trust me. Just like I love you to death. As long as you go get me my fucking book right now."

"What do you need the book for?"

"Liam!"

There, under a cloth flooring in the tire compartment of the trunk, is the book. Alondra's been looking over my shoulder the whole time. When she sees it, she nods with a grin, as if she guessed it was there.

But then she snatches the book right out of my hands! I grapple for her wrist, but she slips out of my fingers, running away, laughing hysterically. She bolts to the front of my car, holding it with two hands, giggling. Then she starts shadowing me, ready to go right if I go left, left if right, as if we're playing tag.

"You promised!"

All the while she's bursting into uncontrollable laughter, just like she and her dad were doing during dinner last night. Now I know where she got her sense of humor from.

She finally lets me approach. She hands me the book then surprises me by throwing her arms around me. I laugh as she kisses my face and lips like crazy.

"Now...what?"

"Can you hold the bag, babe?" she asks, backing up and staring into my eyes. She runs her hand through my hair. "It's kinda heavy. We've gotta walk far to get where we're going."

"Where are we going?"

But she doesn't answer, of course.

So I heave the black duffel bag over my shoulder and hold Alondra's hand, and we parallel the fence at the bottom of a wild grass hill.

It's then that I realize that Alondra has been here before. She seems to know exactly where she's going. My eyes are adjusting too. Shadows are forming along the bushes and trees. Unlike Hawthorne Forest's thick trees, this forest is full of grassy weeds and bushes.

"Oh look, Lee, a cow! She's so cute. Come on, girl."

A brown cow stops right by the barbed-wire fence. Alondra pets its brown hide. But I keep staring at my book, now tucked under her arm.

"I love farms," she says, still petting the cow. "You know,

after my parents died, I moved out of our house and lived on the farm in Flintwood as a girl. It was only after high school in Flintwood that I moved back to the house. Farms are like witches. They're all about loving animals, trees, grass, and Mother Nature. I love that so much. Dad has a few cows and horses, and I used to name all of them when I was a little girl. Isn't this one cute? Now that Dad met you, we should both come and visit the farm. It goes on for miles. And Dad is such an amazing guy."

"He really is."

"He likes you a lot. Don't worry. You always worry about everything so much." She stops petting the animal and points further down the fence. "Come on. Let's go get to the gate and get this break-in over with."

"Break-in!"

The gate to the metal fence looks like it's about fifty yards away. When we reach the gate, a small padlock on a chain blocks our way.

"Open the bag and take out the bolt cutter."

"Bolt cutter! Wait a second. Are you for real, Alondra? We're really going to break through this fence?"

"I told you we were. Hey, I might be mysterious, but I always tell you the truth." She laughs. "Don't worry. Just cut the damn chain."

And she gestures to the duffel bag. Then she hands me a small key.

But I just stare at her.

When I don't obey, she sighs, trades my book for the key, and bends her knees to open the small lock on the bag. She unzips the bag and takes out two-handed cutters. She offers them to me. When I don't take them, she shrugs and positions the cutters directly over the small metal chain.

"Oops," she says, easily snapping the chain. Then she lifts the latch over the gate. I look down into the bag and see what's so heavy. There are two large shovels inside.

"Wait." I snatch her arm. "Why are we trespassing, Alondra?"

"Just stealing dirt. The only thing the owner will care about is a broken cheap padlock. Doubt the cows are going to break through with the latch closed, so the owners are only out ten bucks. After we get this over with, we'll go back home. We're not robbing a bank, babe."

"But *what* are we digging?"

She hesitates. Her lovely pale face gazes up at the moon. It seems even paler under the moonlight, as she turns pensive for a moment.

"Goofer dust."

That, of course, means absolutely nothing to me. And she knows it. That's why she's smiling smugly.

"Goofer dust?"

She nods.

Then she digs into the bag and grabs two large flashlights, handing me one. She zips up the bag and tucks the small key in her pants pocket. I haul the bag back over my shoulder.

"Goofer dust," she repeats. "Liam, didn't you notice we're near Geneva Forest? Winona's house is only a couple miles from here. Ever since the attack on our house, I've been having dreams that we were back in that horrible haunted house. Dreams lead to a powerful connection with Hecate. See, I think the book was the gateway, but not the source of magical power during the attack on our house. My dreams keep showing me the Grant home. You recall how evil that little girls' house was?"

"How can I forget?"

A cow moos. The animal's approaching again.

"*Aww.* Look, Lee. She's following us so that I can pet her again."

"Or she's excited to escape."

Alondra rolls her eyes. Then she closes the latch on the gate behind us.

"See, the trouble with demons," she continues, petting the cow, "is their energy sticks. I think someone is still using the negative energy from that house. The house, like your book, is being channeled. If I get goofer dust around the grounds of that demon house, I can take that back home and perform a ritual in Hawthorne. That'd be a heck of a lot more acceptable to the Grant family than performing magic on their grounds. You remember Alice and Maybelle's house last year? We helped the family, but you and Jane were so mad at me when we scared the hell out of them. Remember? So we're gathering dirt so that we can cast spells *away* from Melanie's family this time. And my house is my hallowed grounds, so I'll have more control. Get it?"

"I guess."

"I really love how you're smart enough to keep up with all this magic stuff, babe," she says, running her hand down my arm. "I really love you."

"Sure, Allie. But shouldn't we be digging the dirt up from the house then?"

"No. I just told you, we don't need to frighten them. We've done enough to that family. Anyway, it's best to collect goofer dust in cemeteries. Kenosha and I came here last year to prepare for the exorcism—you know, Kenosha, that evil voodoo-bitch who possessed you? See, voodoo witches collect grave dirt all the time when practicing magic. Kenosha suggested last year that we collect goofer dust to use in that wicked house. And we did. It proved to work in a powerful ritual back home. So here I'm doing it again."

"I don't see graves."

"Up the hill, smarty."

Well, there goes all her mystery. But now that I understand, I really don't feel any better.

We climb the grassy hill.

When we make it to the hilltop, I see the burial grounds. It looks like a very old burial ground, with wild grass and a few small trees overlooking the surrounding woods. Up here, we can see for miles in all directions. Most of the tombstones have been knocked over. Other stones are broken into pieces. That's when I get why Alondra brought flashlights. Here, away from the road and the farmhouse lights, even under bright moonlight, it's really dark.

"Kenosha and I thought this cemetery dated back to pre–Civil War times," she says. "It was abandoned, but probably survived being high on this hilltop in the middle of nowhere. I researched the area when we were trying to help those girls. Down where we parked, a flood destroyed nearly everything two hundred years ago. Nobody takes care of the place, probably because the whole area was abandoned after the flood. I don't even think the farmhands know this cemetery exists anymore. Kenosha told me she used divination to find the spot."

"Which grave are you going to dig up?"

"I'm not sure," she says, shaking her head and stopping me. We put the bag down on the grass, and she rummages through it again. "I told you, I'm not a voodoo witch, but I feel like if I do a rite with your book, I'll find the right spot. Unfortunately, we're gonna have to do a lot of digging. It's best to grab soil closest to the casket. See, in many funeral rites, people throw dirt over the casket. That's the part that's full of magical intent. But, like I told you, this cemetery is centuries old, and all that magical intent has been buried by lots of non-magical soil. So, lots of digging, I'm afraid, babe."

"And if we're discovered?"

"We'll probably get arrested."

She smiles whimsically. Then she hands me a shovel. And then she just looks into my eyes.

"Don't do that," I say.

"Don't do what?"

"Don't stare at me like that. You're hypnotizing me with

your eyes. You're probably casting a spell on me to make me stupidly agree to do all this digging with you."

"No hypnosis," she says. "We call that love." Then she stands up on her tippy toes and kisses me on my lips again. "Now dig, hero. Dig. If you don't, it's just gonna take me longer."

"Show me where," I say with a sigh.

But she doesn't know. She surveys each tombstone, walking slowly around the creepy broken-down graves. She pauses and weirdly closes her eyes, lifting her palm over some of the gravestones.

Shaking her head, she heads back to the duffel bag and pulls out two sticks. They're connected. She points a stick at each tombstone. Then she reaches for the book I'm carrying under my arm. Even now I'm hesitant to hand it to her. But I do. Then, before one of the granite stones, one rubbed out and difficult to read, she kneels on my grimoire, *Broomstick*. She bobs her head with her eyes closed. She raises the sticks horizontally over the ground again.

"*Quaero.*"

The word seems to be whispered all around the hillside.

I step back when Allie opens her eyes. They're fully white, just like Melanie's were in the guest room that night.

"*Quaero. Quaero familia. Mitch and Kathy Grant. Winona and Melanie. For familia. For familia. Adiuva nos? Adiuva nos?*"

She shuts her eyes and bobs her head up and down.

Then she stands up and wanders around the cliffside, traipsing slowly by each and every tombstone. It's almost like she's in a trance, possessed, a ghost, or someone sleepwalking. But she keeps striking the air and holding those two sticks horizontally over the ground. Finally she hovers over one of the broken tombstones. The date etched on the stone is 1823. I can't make out much of anything else. Here she forms the symbol of a cross, with the sticks, before her chest.

She picks up *Broomstick* and places it near this stone.

"We strike ground here, Liam," she mutters. She looks up and, thankfully, her eyes are jade again. "This is the best place."

She takes a shovel and starts digging grass and weeds. And before you know it, I'm joining her in another one of her crazed escapades.

"Can you get two glass jars out of the bag, hun?"

"I don't know how I get into this stuff with you."

"Have you looked in the mirror lately?" she asks, shoveling. "Lucius was right. You're a warlock. We might not have initiated you, but you still are very much a witch. You even apply your dark gothic makeup every morning. Remember when you swore to me you were never going to do that? You're not initiated," she says as her shovel clangs against mine, "but you're still very much a witch, Liam."

She stops digging about a foot down.

"Okay," she says, taking a deep breath. "That's enough. I'm deep enough to reach the original hallowed ground, I think. Just open the two jars and put them under me, and I'll shuffle the dirt in with my shovel."

"And that's it?"

"What more did you expect?" She laughs. "Thought I'd open the casket?"

"Yeah, and I figured I'd see lightning and hear thunder too."

She shrugs.

She carefully turns the shovel over one of the jars, filling it with grave dirt. When it's full, I stick the other empty jar under her and she fills that one too. She screws the jars shut and tosses them in the bag. And then we cover the grave with dirt again. After we pat the ground with our shovels, she throws her shovel in the bag. Then she tosses my shovel and *Broomstick* in the bag too.

"Easy-peasy." And she claps her hands together, brushing off dirt. "But we better go, babe. The farmhands could have planted cameras."

"Cameras!"

She laughs. Then she comes real close and puts her arms around me.

"Come here. Kiss me. Thanks for putting up with me, lover."

"You said this will help fix our house?"

"I sure hope so," she says with a shrug. And then we're at it again smooching. "Umm, love me. That's so nice."

It is. Under the light of the full moon, it feels romantic. And in our embrace, in the cold night, she feels warm.

We're so high up. This plateau is likely the tallest peak in the whole area. If I knew where to look down among the trees, I might be able to spot Winona's hell house below. I can't see the farm or road from here, but on the other side, down a slightly steeper slope than the one we came from, is a shadowed land of trees. Thousands of them.

I love holding Allie and just kissing her like this. I think I could do it till sunrise.

She slides off her leather jacket and reaches for my coat. Then she raises my T-shirt and rubs my stomach and chest. Her fingers gliding over my skin feel wonderful. But it's cold.

Somehow we find ourselves on the ground only about a foot away from the mound of dirt we dug up. I reach under her shirt. Then my hands make their way up to her bra, and then under, touching her breasts. She leans into me as I brush a finger over her nipple. But then her body shakes. She's too cold. That only makes me clutch her more tightly.

"What are we doing?" I mutter.

"Making out in a cemetery," she whispers. "It's hot."

"It's public."

"Hotter."

"You suggested cameras."

"Let 'em watch."

"And sinful. This isn't just hallowed ground, it's consecrated ground."

But she shrugs and pulls up her black T-shirt. Then she

unlatches her bra from behind. And now her pale breasts shine white under the moonlight. It's nothing I haven't seen. We had sex earlier this afternoon back home. We seem to be making love every day. But there's something about doing it here, outdoors under the white moonlight, that feels surreal. Especially when she gazes back at me with those amazing hypnotic eyes. Or maybe it's because we're making out in a cemetery?

She's all over me now, on top, kissing me with those soft lips and rubbing her breasts along my chest. She pulls at my shirt, and I fall back, my skin brushing against the wild grass, dirt, and rocks. Then she yanks down her pants and underwear. I rub the soft skin around her waist and then her ass. And I squeeze her close.

"I've been waiting for this," she says quietly. "I've wanted to make love to you ever since we got out of the car. Sorry, but I'm madly in love with you. I just can't resist. The stars and the moon are our ceiling. The goddess Diana is inviting. And it's just you and me alone together tonight."

She unzips my pants and tugs them down. Then she pulls out my cock and strokes it.

In moonlight, I gaze into her eyes. Those amazing bright eyes. She smiles. And she smells nice. I love her perfume. It's always woodsy and natural and it mixes well with the smell of the dirt and grass.

"You're absolutely crazy," I reply with a nervous laugh. "Do you...do you know that?"

"But you want me, right?" Her lips gently touch mine before I can answer. All the while, she keeps stroking my cock. "And... you want to fuck me, right? You love me," she says between kisses on my lips. "My mystery. My secrets. My magic. You love this witch. Don't you? Make love to her. Show her. Right here and now. Come on. Under the stars and the moon, fuck her. Is it so wrong? I think it'll be amazing. And...is it wrong when two people are madly in love with one another, wherever they are? We have the chance to do it under the stars of Astraeus and

Selene tonight alone on a hilltop. Why should we stop when we both want that?"

She strokes my cock while running her lips gently over mine again. Our tongues dance as she gently tugs at my upper lip.

"Do you...want me?"

"Yes."

So she straddles me. Then, taking me inside, she moves up and down gently.

And we're doing it. We're making love outdoors under the full moonlight. It's not the first time we've done it outside. We've made love in her backyard. But it is the first time we've done this publicly. She's right. It feels amazing. Is it because it's wrong? Is it so wrong to make love in an old broken-down graveyard?

With her naked breasts shining in the moonlight, she rocks up and down over me, closing her eyes, while rubbing my chest.

She opens her eyes and smiles.

But then she shakes. She's cold. So I pull her waist closer to me, so much tighter, just to warm her. She responds with a moan. But her body still shakes.

"Allie," I mutter, "you're getting too cold. We have to stop to get you warm."

"Warm me."

She lies over me as she continues to gently move her hips up and down. Moving faster now. Her breasts are pressed against my hard chest. I run my hand down to finger their curves. All the while she keeps moving up and down below, faster and faster. I touch her back and glide my fingers down to the crack of her ass, squeezing her even closer. And she moans.

Then she stops. Because we hear voices.

"Someone's coming!" she snaps, jumping out of my embrace.

Both of us search the hillside. She snatches her jacket to cover herself. I grab my coat.

Two strangers in hooded forest-green robes, holding shovels, slowly make their way up to the top of the hill.

"I should have known," one of them quips. I recognize that infernal voice. It's Kenosha, that bitch-witch who possessed me last year with her Ekimmu demon spell.

She removes her hood, revealing her bald dark-skinned head. She has a bunch of gold earrings on both ears and a string of golden necklaces. Her friend is dark-skinned too, wearing the same green robe, but when she lifts her hood, I see she has long black hair, more like Alondra. And Kenosha's companion seems younger.

"Consecrating this hallowed ground, witches?" asks the younger witch.

"Just an Abaddon witch with her male escort, Clotho," Kenosha answers. "Apparently Kathy contacted you, Alondra?" Then she turns to me. "And you're actually still hanging with her, Liam? After everything that you saw at her house. She nearly killed me and the headmaster. Remember? Why stay with this monster?"

"*I was possessed by you!*"

"*Lamias!*" Alondra yells. "*You're fucking lamias! Keep away from us!*"

But Kenosha just stands over us, shaking her head, with folded arms. But really, standing over us like this, not giving us privacy while we're still half-naked, is probably the best way to piss us off more.

"I was the one who suggested we collect dust here last year," says Kenosha. "Do you even know what the hell you're doing, Falconsong? Collecting dirt in a cemetery is voodoo witchcraft. You don't practice vodun. You practice Wicca mixed with the sickest forms of Thelemic Crowley sex magic."

"I already collected the dirt," Alondra snaps. "I have two jars. Would you like to borrow one?"

Clotho actually turns to Kenosha as if she'd consider it. I don't blame her. I mean, who wants to dig in the cemetery in the middle of the night?

"How did you know we would be here?" I ask.

"We didn't, Liam," Kenosha says. "Kathy called—"

"*Scram!*" Alondra shouts. "Never mind. I don't want to give you two shit! Go dig your own goofer dust." Then, with them just still standing and staring, Allie turns crazy. "*You two lamias mind fucking turning the fuck around? We have to get dressed, a'ight? I tell you, Liam, these two are lamias. Their whole goddamn coven in New Orleans is full of fucking blood-sucking vampires. They accuse me of evil, but they hide in a bush to watch us fuck.*"

"What's a lamia?" I ask.

"A vampire that eats little children, Lee," Kenosha says irritatingly calmly. "Like the demon Lilith. Alondra is basically describing herself. She's talking about Alondra Billington."

"I'm talking 'bout you, bitch! The headmaster, you, Ariel here, and the rest of all you witch-hypocrites from your stupid-ass witch council."

"Do you at least still guard Escoba's grimoire, Liam?" Kenosha asks with a sigh. "Please tell me you didn't already give the book to her?"

But Alondra gestures for them to turn around again. They finally turn. Then Allie grabs the rest of my clothes and tosses me my shirt.

I jump up and quickly throw it on.

"When did Kathy contact you?" Kenosha asks.

"Fuck off, a'ight?" Alondra says. "She didn't."

"Then how did you know to come here again?"

"Melanie appeared in my room," I say.

"What?" Kenosha asks, whirling around. "You saw that girl again?"

"If he says he did," Alondra remarks dismissively, "he did. But the girl's only seven, or something."

"Going on ten," Kenosha says. "And I've found enough magic still in that house to charge a baby."

"Don't talk to them, Lee," Alondra says. "She and her whole fucking Crescent coven are fucking lamias."

"Liam, please," Kenosha persists. "We're here because Kathy fears for her life. All the noises in the house are back. She said that one night, the shouting was so bad that she and Mitch ran out of their bedroom to find Melanie in a trance at the bottom of the stairs, maybe sleepwalking, holding a knife. She was speaking gibberish. Mitch and Kathy yelled for her to drop the knife. Mitch ended up being pushed down the stairs by some invisible force."

"You guys infused that house with evil," Alondra snaps.

"That's why we're here," Kenosha says. "I accept the blame. Sure. But right now, for the sake of the family, it doesn't matter. I want to help them."

"It does matter. You cast—"

"Stop and listen to me for once, Alondra!" Kenosha exclaims. "Kathy said that she saw Winona lying on the ceiling in a panic with her younger sister, Melanie, pointing up and laughing at her. Your vision was real, Liam. That little girl, Melanie, is possessed by goetia. It might just be Melanie this time."

"Because you brought demons into the house, bitch!" shouts Alondra.

"Who cares who's to blame, Hawthorne Witch?" asks Clotho calmly. "We shouldn't fight. We have to consider the family. That girl needs to be exorcised if she's possessed. We need to help her."

"My house is being attacked because of your voodoo mumbo jumbo!" Alondra snaps. "For all I know, you guys are using a poor girl to attack us."

"We must work together," Clotho says, shaking her head. "You two might hate each other now, but that poor family is suffering."

"I think Melanie's casting," I say with a nod.

"Oh fuck, Lee!" Alondra snaps, opening her eyes wide. "Fuck! Stay quiet." She runs her fingers through her long hair. Then she zips up my duffel bag. She hooks her arm into mine and throws the bag over her shoulder. "Let's get the hell out of here." Alondra sticks up her middle finger at them. "We've entertained them long enough."

"I went to the house this morning, Alondra," Kenosha says. She talks more quickly because we're already leaving. "Melanie's catatonic. I believe she's in a trance after ritualistic magic. Could she be in shock over her father? Sure. But how can witchcraft not be to blame for his fall? Melanie held a ceremonial athame. Kathy showed it to me. Apparently, the girls found the knife in the house when they first moved in."

"Both kids found a grimoire before High Priestess appeared," Clotho adds. "The house was cursed not only by Willow, but by ceremony done by evil witches practicing black magic before us."

"Your High Priestess fucking attacked their family, Ariel," says Alondra, cocking her head back. We're already heading down the hill. "Talk to her about ruining the family. And consider following someone else."

"We need to tell them about Lucius, Allie," I say.

"*Shut up, Lee!*" Alondra cries, yanking back my elbow and staring into my eyes. "*Fuck, I mean it! Keep out of all this!*"

"*Lucius*, Liam?" asks Kenosha, opening her eyes wide too. "Lucius Campbell, Alondra? I thought Dr. Campbell was still teaching devil worship in Birmingham, England? Is he in the States now?"

"Ha, how would I know?"

"Tell me more, Liam," Kenosha says.

"Keep your mouth shut, Liam," Allie warns.

"We need to work together," Clotho says with a nod.

"Well, I don't want to work with them, Clotho," Kenosha

says, shaking her head. "Alondra is convinced that demonic sex magic is the way to perform proper ritual. She's probably moving on now to murder or infanticide. You tell me? Liam, do you think you're kissing her in a cemetery by mistake? Or that she drew you here just for a hug? Alondra believes that sinful ceremonial magic in a cemetery amplifies her magical power. And what better way to empower the dust than to have sex with you—"

"*How dare you!*" Alondra rages. She rushes back up the hill toward Kenosha. Kenosha backs away from Alondra's fury.

"Guys, stop!" Clotho is pulling Kenosha back from her.

But then there's a whistle and a dog barking farther down the hill.

"*Who's there!*" cries a stranger.

"Shit," Alondra says in a forced whisper, looking around the hillside. "Shit! Thanks a lot, losers. Now we've been discovered!"

Alondra rushes back down to me, this time tugging me into a run. I grab the heavy bag from her.

Racing down the opposite side of the hill, I nearly slide on some mud, but Allie helps me up. It's rough rushing down the slope with the heavy duffel bag on my shoulder. Willow and Clotho trail behind. All the while, the dog is still barking.

"Can't you cast magic or something to stop them?" I ask.

"Sometimes...it's better to run," Alondra says, panting.

"My car's on the other side of the hill, Allie," I say.

"We're parked down this side," says Kenosha, not far behind us. "We can drive you back to your car."

"The hell with you two," Alondra says.

"I say let 'em drive us," I say.

"If they hate each other this much..." Clotho says, out of breath, catching up to me. "You and I can drive back to your car and pick her up. But I don't know how we're going to dig for grave dirt up there now, High Priestess."

"You can have some of ours," I suggest.

"The hell they can!" snaps Alondra. "God, stop being so damn nice all the time!"

8

MY WARNING

Being close to Ostara—that's "Easter" in witch-lingo—the weather in Hawthorne is warming. So it's nice enough for me to spend the afternoon studying on a bench on our grassy hilltop, overlooking campus, near the student center. And being perched up on a green grassy hilltop away from the woods, this is the absolute best place to study. It's a couple of acres of lawn with scattered trees—surrounded by the forest, of course—sort of like an artificially made glade or a huge version of Alondra's backyard. It's college-made, but even with the planted trees and lawn, the birds perched on branches with their birdsong soothe me. Below this awesome expanse lies the center of Hawthorne University with our concrete main thoroughfare between brick buildings. It's the best view of campus. After I grabbed a pretzel from a vendor and headed up the hill for a cup of coffee, I quickly left my books on this bench just to reserve it. This real estate goes fast on a nice day like today.

So that's what I'm doing now—quite happy about it, to tell you the truth. I'm sipping a cup of joe and chewing on a pretzel, while reviewing notes on, ironically, Bill's lecture: Sister Concezione and her devil letter.

What a weird whacked-out tale of demon possession. But

you can imagine this gothic stuff being right up Bill's alley. Story goes that Sister Concezione lived in a convent in Palma di Montechiaro in Sicily in the seventeenth century. Occasionally, when praying before the altar, she claimed to hear the voice of Satan. But that was nothing compared with what happened next. One night, her hallucinations became explosive. And that morning, her fellow sisters found her on the floor of her room, face and hands covered in black ink, clutching papers.

She claimed she had been possessed and had written a letter in a sleepwalking trance. It was thought to be scribbled in a special language of the devil. A psychotic break in a schizophrenic or bipolar sufferer? Maybe. The nun was known to have linguistic skills, and the devil's language seemed to be a mix of familiar languages like Italian and Greek. Or maybe her devil possession was real? Maybe it was a Sumerian Ekimmu? Look, I suppose after everything I've been through, I'm the last one to propose that the poor nun didn't experience a real demonic possession.

I could have reviewed the devil letter with the lecturer, in Billy's apartment, I suppose. But my friend is way too excited over his planned initiation into Alondra's coven this Friday. Yeah, not only are they going to try to cast a spell with grave dirt, they're planning on finally initiating my best friend. Bill's on cloud nine.

I tear off another piece of salty delight while taking a deep breath. Then I look down over the amazing view of campus again.

And then... I feel like that mad nun meeting the devil in the seventeenth century. Because far below, along the main drag of campus—amid students with backpacks, a bicyclist riding illegally down the walkway, and two gray-haired professors holding books—I catch a motley trio heading up to the grassy hillside. Everyone's glancing at them, mainly because of the guy in the middle. He's like Sister Concezione's Satan—bald with a goatee, dressed in black, wearing a black cape with a red satin interior, and holding a cane. I don't know what the cane's about. He's not using it to help him walk; he's just sort of twirling it as he walks. The other two are also wearing all black. Cline's in black suspenders over a dark gray T-shirt and black pants, while Silvia is in a black shirt and skirt. And they are all wearing dark gothic makeup, like me. But even in Hawthorne, where gothic makeup is in, these three bohemians look strange.

The girl at the pretzel stand stares as they saunter by. Then I catch a young kid holding a skateboard turning and looking back at them.

I tear another piece from my salty pretzel. But somehow it's not that appetizing anymore.

That's when they spot me. Silvia waves, her hand held really high, with a grin, happy-go-lucky as always. The other two keep their stoic expressions. But the weirdest thing is I'm going to have to wait. They still have to exit the main concrete walkway and make their way up the grassy glade.

That means I could bolt. Should I? They're obviously not here for a lecture. Nor are they coming to the student store to buy books.

Fuck.

I take a deep breath instead. Then I throw my stapled notes in Dr. Kriegel's occult textbook. I stand up, preparing to turn and walk down the meandering sidewalk across the lawn. If I walk fast enough, I could still ditch them.

They reach the lawn.

"Hey, Lee!" shouts Silvia, waving excitedly again. "Don't you be going nowhere!"

And...shit. I just freeze, holding my books under my arm like a dork.

"Hi, Silvia."

"The doctor wants to talk to you," Silvia adds. "Ain't it absolutely fabulous?"

Lucius infernally nods. Cline just keeps scowling at her

surroundings, as if the campus is annoying to her. Everything always seems to annoy her.

"Liam," Lucius says. He nods again. "Blessed be. May you never thirst, initiate."

When they are finally close enough, I gesture at the bench. A wood table is behind me. But first, Lucius gives me his hand to shake. Silvia embraces me. Cline just ignores me, staring at the ground.

Then all three sit on the opposite side of the bench.

"I see you finally got a chance to visit my college?" I quip.

"Indeed," Lucius says with a nod. "It's quite quaint. Small and quaint. Nice though."

Well, that sounds insulting.

"I totally love it, Lumi," says Silvia. I notice for the first time she's chewing gum. "It's so fab, ain't it? I think I should apply here. What do you think, Cline? I could go here after community college. Right?"

"You'd never have the grades, girl," Cline says, rolling her eyes.

"Bitch," Silvia replies with a scowl. Then she sticks her tongue out, revealing the white gum she's been chewing. So she rolls the gum back in her mouth. Then she grins at me again, reaching over and touching my hand.

"I love it, Liam. I really love it. It kind of reminds me of your guru. The whole school is, like, totally the woods. It's like nature and it's totally dope."

"Thanks, Silvia."

"It does well for Alondra and her coven, doesn't it?" asks Lucius with a nod. "Liam, allow me to get to the point. This week is our last sabbath in Hawthorne before my order returns home to Raleigh. We will be heading back on Monday. As you know, my order—"

"I'm not giving you the book."

He nods.

"I told you I swore to keep it away from Allie in ceremony."

He nods again.

"Listen to our god and stop fucking interrupting him," snaps Cline. "Shut up and let him finish."

She seems to be the complete opposite of Silvia. And, in fact, Silvia scowls at her again.

"I came to warn you, warlock," Lucius says. "Over the years, after countless ritualistic trances, I've seen blessed Androgyne here develop a talent for prophecy." He gestures to Cline. Apparently Androgyne is Cline's cult name. "I've learned to trust her intuition and her ability to predict the future, not only in divination, but in her ability to interpret tarot. Most recently, she has prophesied danger. She predicts that a powerful maga will attempt to curse you on the night of our ritual this Friday —whether you join us or not. It is my belief that necromancy has been at work in this town over the past few moons. But now, if blessed Androgyne is right—and, as I said, she always is —Friday's planned conjuring on Falconsong's hallowed ground, between our two circles, could provide your enemy precisely the energies needed to harm you.

"We all know of the attack earlier on your house. Because of your reluctance to learn our craft, it's my belief that it's only because of your close association with Alondra that things have not turned out badly for you. *Yet.* Alondra shields you from the offender's curse on her hallowed ground. Still—" He raises his index finger. "Friday marks a problem. We seek to open the gates of the underworld and use dark energy from both circles, on the shoulders of the unicursal hexagram, to identify precisely who it is who attacks your hallowed ground. I believe we can discover this offender. But by doing so, warlock, I fear that we shall open the flood gates for Ekimmu to gather once more and invade your hallowed ground. Your house."

He pauses. I don't say a damn thing, because I don't even know how to respond to all this. Silvia nods, smacking her gum with a rueful grin.

"You think I'm your adversary?" Lucius asks carefully. "No,

no, this isn't right. I have no interest in causing you harm. I admire the kundalini I feel from your aura, and I look forward to the opportunity to watch the magus within you grow."

"Our God loves all of us, Liam," Silvia says with a nod between smacking her gum. "He's absolutely amazing."

"I don't want to be a witch," I say.

"Being a witch is incontrovertible," Lucius says with a shrug. "You are. In fact, I believe it is dangerous to think otherwise." He quickly raises his palm. "But I came here to deliver Androgyne's warning. That's all. I strongly advise you to accompany us at our last ritual on Friday. You need us to be with you in case things go awry. We can protect you if you join us within the circle."

"Because you want to use my book," I object. "I told Allie I would never join her in ceremony. That's our agreement. The only reason I ever attended one of her meetings was because of my Ekimmu possession."

"What if I told you that you are at risk of possession again if you don't? Consider it, Liam. The decision is yours. It is true that your book would greatly enhance my work, sure, and our casting would be easier with it. But I am trying to tell you that I came here today for *your* benefit, not mine. I am not here to ask for the book." Then he stands up and shrugs. "Good day. My message is delivered. I wish the best of luck to you. I truly mean that. May you be free to do as you please. Be free, as we all are deep inside."

"Hail Satan," Silvia says, bowing her head.

"Hail Satan," Cline echoes with a nod.

"Hail Satan, initiate," Lucius says, bowing his head to me. "And best of luck to you."

Silvia waves, smiling. Cline just looks around, ignoring me, as if the whole encounter was a bother. Then both gothic witches accompany the devil back down the winding sidewalk on our grassy hill.

9

SENSORY PERCEPTION

I'm sitting in Connor Sill Hall, a small lecture hall about a quarter the size of the monstrous lecture hall Allie lectured in, trying to keep my attention on my Psychology of Perception class. The auditorium is a newer addition to our campus, made up of fancy orange swivel chairs and cream-colored walls. But the chairs are empty. It's not really a bad class, just everyone knows Dr. Bruer basically tests right out of the textbook. I debated whether to come to lecture at all, but I need to do anything I can to distract myself from all the shit on my mind. Plus I figured, despite goofer dust and cemeteries, I'm still in school. Aren't I?

"We discussed the process by which a stimulus is detected by the brain," says Dr. Bruer. He's a young lanky guy, not much older than me, who always lectures in gray sweatpants. "This is so very interesting. We'll go through this using our china cabinet in the dining room example again." A picture of a dining room table comes up on a projector screen behind him. "Light from the ceiling reflects down on the wood of the cabinet. That light hits the lens of your eyes, used for focusing, and then passes to the retina. The retina, as we discussed, is built of rods and cones. Cone cells are photoreceptors that detect red, green, or blue. Taken together, the red of the brown table, mixed with *green*, gives you brown. Then that information is collected and transported electrically into the optic section of the brain, at the back of your head. All that occurs in a fraction of a second. That is incredible. Absolutely incredible. Then it's further processed by the thinking section of your brain. The frontal cortex. And, voilà, your mind sees a cabinet."

Fascinating.

I can't focus on all this now. Can you blame me? That devil claimed I'm going to be cursed tonight. I fought with Allie over that again. I told her what Lucius had told me and, of course, she strongly urged me to heed his warning and join them. Then I went crazy shouting that all my problems in Hawthorne are because of her. It's like our same recurrent fight on a broken record being played over and over and over again. She did her usual irritating thing: telling me how I actually love what I hate about her. Man, I got so disturbed that I even called Bill asking if I could spend the night at his place. The invitation's open. But how is that going to stop my problems? Bill's got Alondra's friends visiting him at his place all the time now.

"The brain perceives all this in just a fraction of a second. A fraction of a second. And it's only by metacognition that we even notice..."

I can't care. But you gotta hand it to good ole Dr. Bruer. He lectures with such gusto.

"For the test, you'll want to know about opsin. The cones only respond to three colors through opsin. This is so incredible. So amazing. We see all the colors in the world through only three main colors. The red opsin is sensitive to mid-five-hundred nanometers. This is red light. Then the green ranges lower, closer to five-hundred..."

"Hey, mister?" whispers a young voice in the chair to my left. "Psst. Mister. Can I talk to you for a sec?"

I figure it's a girl wanting to borrow a pen or something. But then I recall the seat to my left was empty. A short girl dressed in a black robe with a hood over her head is beside me. The robe is like a miniature version of our black witch robes.

It's Melanie!

"Can you bring your book over to my house? Please. I really need your help. I want to read it really badly. Mom and Pa are acting a lot like Winnie now. They don't want to move. I thought with your book I might be able to help them move again and not die."

Her eyes glow white under the hood.

"*Vade retro!*"

That makes the little girl laugh.

"And that leads to nine times nine, Liam," lectures Dr. Bruer, with a nod, onstage. "Which, of course, adds up to nine. A fundamental theorem for understanding the perception of our entire world. Nine is always nine. Wouldn't you say? You are absolutely nothing. *Nein. Nein. Nein.*"

I look up, but he's pointing to a slide of a china cabinet projected behind him.

"*Vade retro!*" I shout, hitting my desk. "*Vade retro!*"

A few people in the front row turn, staring at me.

Melanie disappears.

Then I feel really stupid. And all this reminds me of the horror I went through last year when those creepy girls showed up during class.

I thought I was done with all this!

Gruffly, I gather my notebook and pen and stuff them in my backpack. Then I quickly make my way down the empty aisle and through the door.

It's raining outside. That's Georgia weather for you. This morning it was hot, now it's raining. Making my way through the impromptu drizzle, I clap along a wet cement walkway, rushing around a trailer classroom, to the back parking lot. Then I throw open the door to my Camaro.

But I don't turn on the ignition. I just sit inside my car

watching the rain fall on my windshield, feeling totally freaked out.

10

THE ABYSS

It's dark despite the six lit red candles surrounding me. I can't see much of anything except an occasional flicker of candlelight against the walls of my room. *Broomstick* lies on my lap. I don't recall when I returned and set up these candles, or when I created the hexagram by pouring chalk under me, or even when I brought my book in from outside. I'm not even sure where I got the white chalk. The girls use chalk to encircle their bonfire sometimes, I suppose. I think there's a bag in the backyard? Did I fetch that and pour it on the carpet in the guest room? My last memory is turning off the TV, with the Braves losing, and heading to the guest room.

What the hell did I do after watching the baseball game? Did I say my goodbyes to the rest of the gang in the living room, like I normally do before they go off to their ceremony? And did I see that weirdo Lucius and his scarlet motley crew arrive?

All I recall is a deep unsettling fear ever since seeing Melanie in class again. A horror. I still feel it.

I feel so afraid.

Lucius warned me about being cursed. Well, I don't trust him. Honestly, if anybody's cursing me, it's probably him.

Was it fear that made me arrange these candles and the

symbol on the floor? Am I performing a spell? Or is this all another illusion from the book? Did I open and start reading *Broomstick* again? Is the book making me do this?

I touch the ground with my right palm. Then I touch my chest with my left and lift two fingers to the ceiling. Taking a deep breath, calming myself, closing my eyes tight, I center myself in the fashion you taught me, teacher. And then... I steady my breathing.

"*Verumtamen oculus tuis videbis. Verumtamen oculus tuis videbis. Verumtamen oculus tuis videbis.*"

I AM STANDING IN A LARGE FIELD OF WILD GRASS. IT IS LIKE THE grass in Allie's backyard, only the wild grass here goes on and on forever in all directions. All I see is tall green and brown grass up to my ankles under a brilliant yellow sun in a cerulean sky, patched with sporadic wisps of white. The blue surrounds me over every horizon. But despite sky and green grass, I still *feel* the carpet under my legs as I sit cross-legged on the guest room floor, meditating before my grimoire, *Broomstick*.

My breath becomes steadier.

Cautiously I advance over reddish-brown dust. Looking down, I see that the grass under my bare feet has been replaced by this fine dust. Like Martian dirt. I'm traipsing upon it along a narrow ravine. When I look up, the yellow sunlight blinds me. But the sunlight is only coming from over my right shoulder. To my left is a rocky wall. But I can also gaze down. Far below a sheer cliff, far, far below, I see crashing waves.

I hear nothing.

I raise my head again and gaze around at the six flickering candles encircling me in my guest room. On the wall, I see blurring balls of light—multicolored shapes that fade in and out of my vision. I realize something I had never realized before. All vision is made up of these blotches of colored lights.

And without the blotches beyond my vision lies absolutely nothing. By the center of my vision is zero.

Nein.

The air is still, dry, and warm.

I run my fingers over the rough, rocky wall to my left and continue touching it, as if my fingertips will keep me steady and prevent my fall from the precipice. My shaky bare feet cling to the ground. I have to practically walk toe to heel over the very narrow bluff to avoid falling.

In the flickering light to my right, shapes emerge, like rays of colored light cut by a prism into rainbows. Like the balls of light in my room, these shapes create forms: female forms, naked breasts and naked hips swaying to a drumbeat. It's an arousing erotic dance of rainbow light. But the figures must be dancing on thin air, for they dance fifty yards out, where there's no ground beneath them.

Far below, the waves turn red, like blood. A bloody red sea rages beneath me.

The figures are light. And that's what the light from my candles is. Light. Like the energy of the sun, the moon and the sky. As above, so below. Earth, fire, wind, water, spirit. *Gnosis. Verumtamen oculus tuis videbis. Verumtamen. Verumtamen.*

Light spins along a dark tunnel. I am the center.

A solitary figure in red dances before me. Every move of her naked arm or leg blurs like rays of color. And a drumbeat plays on. I squint, attempting to discern the woman dancing before me. She waves her arms up high in the air, dips them down, and then rises again as if bowing to some god. But then a light as bright as the sun burns everything.

I'm on my precipice again, my feet dangling over the sheer drop of over a thousand feet. The trail is now too narrow to transverse. I'm trapped. I can no longer move. And I have no choice other than to either freeze and remain motionless or take a leap unto death.

I am the observer and the actor. Once there was water; now

there is an endless abyss. The sun above brings forth all the dark shadows below. For without the sun and soul, there is absolutely nothing. Zero. *Nein.*

Verumtamen oculus tuis videbis. Verumtamen oculus tuis videbis. Verumtamen oculus tuis videbis.

∼

"NOT OF AIR. NOT OF FEATHER. NOT OF DIRT. THIS LION IS FIRE. Jumbee took the mind of a child. Mambo Escoba comes to help reclaim it. You. I. Abbie is not here to help falcon nor half moon. I come for my daughters. Bring my daughters to me. Save them. Save the child of my blood. If you fail, she may yet quell the confused mind. Not of falcon nor of half moon. Only with my flame can you know what Ougu does. Burn. Burn. Burn. Light a fire that reveals shadows. Save your daughters and you save Hawthorne. Save your daughters and you save me and yourself."

Igni. Igni. Igni!

The door to my room creaks open. I'm terrified it will be that little demon-girl, Melanie. But a dark-skinned woman in a white headdress and robe stands on the threshold with her head down.

"As they dance and howl at the moon," she says quietly, "do you see my work, Oungan? All those witches cannot do what you do. They are of the earth, but you, Oungan, are of fire. Light my fire. I close my eyes. You close your eyes. But I open yours with a blindfold. And then, when you open your eyes again, what do you see?"

"Who are you?"

"All those witches dancing outside," she says, gesturing behind her, "dancing around the fire creating darkness, you hold the light. Refuse me, all goes and you forfeit your life by jumbee; accept me, become a priest, and then our daughters survive in victory after dawn."

"I don't want to be a witch."

"Not for falcon, or half moon, but for the daughters you must be reborn."

"Who are you?"

"Escoba Hawthorne."

She finally raises her head. The dark-skinned witch gazes upon me with a serene countenance. She's not scary, she seems calm, kind of the way I remember Agnes, the headmaster of the council. But this is a ghost, according to Alondra. Escoba died two hundred years ago.

"How are you here?" I ask.

"You opened my book, Cadence Hawthorne."

I touch my eyes and feel a blindfold. That freaks me out.

All turns dark. Of course, because I have a cloth tied over my eyes. How could I see anything with this covering?

But in darkness, I hear words whispered by a thousand voices: *Verumtamen oculus tuis videbis. Verumtamen oculus tuis videbis. Verumtamen oculus tuis videbis.*

"Step away from the stairs!" shouts Kathy. *"My god, step away, Winnie! Keep away from the stairs! Melanie's going to make you fall!"*

I'm upstairs in that demon house in Geneva Forest again. Winona's house. The lights are on, but it's very dim. The windows are dark downstairs too, so it must be evening. Mitch keeps pulling at a little girl in a white nightgown. I recognize the girl at the top of the stairs as Winona. Mitch is trying to stop his daughter from tumbling down. But Winona seems to want to fall, continuously pushing off her dad and pulling him downward.

At the foot of the stairs stands Melanie. She's in a small black robe, like the robes of our coven, looking weird like she did in that perception lecture, staring up at her mom, dad, and sister with creepy pearly-white eyes. But she's shaking—laughing? Or shaking in fear? No...she's definitely laughing. She's gesturing for Winona to come down the stairs. But I know she's not asking her to *walk* down the steps, she wants her sister to fall. And, most ghastly, in Melanie's left hand, the little girl holds a sharp knife. I recognize that as a ceremonial knife, the athame I've seen in Alondra's house.

"*Keep away from the stairs!*" screams her mom, Kathy. "*Just keep away from her, Winona! Your sister is sick in the head!*"

"My god, Winona, stop this!" shouts Mitch. "Stop leaning over the steps. I can't keep holding you back. You're gonna fall!"

"*Melanie, leave your sister alone!*" Mitch hollers.

"Come on down, Winnie!" shouts Melanie, laughing. "Come on. Why don't you play with me no more? Remember our book of stars? And all those cards? Remember when the book made you push me down the stairs? Well, I got something for you. You know what the good book says? Eye for an eye? Come on now—" She covers her left eye with her hand. "And I'll show my one eye. My eye's a *whooole* lot better."

Then Melanie lowers her head to her chest, shaking in laughter.

A flash of lightning lights up the stairway. Thunder rumbles in the house. And I hear torrential rainfall hitting the roof.

"*Drop the knife, Melanie!*" commands Mitch. "*My god, come on, drop it now!*"

"*Stop it, Melanie!*" screams Winona. "*Stop it! It's not funny anymore!*"

"*Stop it, Melanie,*" Melanie shouts back. "*Stop it! They're trying to help you!*"

"Drop the knife now!" orders Mitch. "I mean it. Just drop it now, Melanie!"

"Why don't you come down and fucking get it, Pa?"

Melanie lifts up her sleeve. She draws the blade along her bare skin. A red line forms. Winona screams. Then Melanie licks the blood from her arm and spits it at them. I hear another scream. That's her mother. Kathy collapses on the carpet beside me. And that's followed by a thousand screams seemingly coming from within the walls. Then a wind blows inside the house—*inside*—nearly forcefully enough to knock me down.

"*Sacrificium!*" yells Melanie, opening pearly-white eyes in madness. She raises her bloody arm. She stares up at the ceiling with wild white eyes. "*Sacrificium. Enteritus en sanguim, witches! Make me a witch! Make me a witch! Send me the book and initiate me, Oungan, in all your wholesome bloody glory! Give me your goddamn book, Liam! Hurry up, won't you? See the blood flow beneath you?*" She looks right up at me with her pearly-white eyes. "*Bring it. Bring it on, into my house! So that I can be a fucking cunt-sucking whore, just like your sinner wife!*"

"*What's happening to her!*" screams Winona.

Winona breaks from her father's grasp.

She leaps.

But Mitch somehow catches part of her gown and pulls her back. The force makes her dad slip. It sends Mitch rolling down the stairs.

Lightning bursts forth again. Then thunder seems to shake the foundations of the whole house once more.

Mitch lands at Melanie's feet, unconscious. Melanie, eyes open wide, head shaking, lips twitching, just gazes down at her fallen dad.

"THAT'S JUST HOW IT HAPPENED, LIAM," whispers MELANIE'S voice in my ear. Her voice quivers. "Yeah. That's just how. Please come and help us. Please. Come over and bring your book so that Momma, Winnie, and me can read it. 'Fraid it might be too late, but I still want to try and help Pa with your book of stars."

"Take the High Priestess's athame," says a woman's voice sternly in total darkness. This isn't Escoba's voice. It's a stranger. "Cut your arm and bleed. Bleed and you shall be reborn. You wish to be initiated? Cut yourself. Initiate yourself or the scarlet harlot will strike you down in her revelation of dark gnosis."

But the last thing I want is to be initiated as a witch. So I reach up and touch the cloth tied around my head.

"*Do not remove your blindfold,*" demands the stranger.

"Initiate yourself for protection, Oungan," says Escoba's voice more calmly. "Or Jumbee be coming for you. Either jump or remain standing. Trapped souls die. Don't pass now to Abbie's Summerland. My daughters need you to be alive."

"Psst, mister?" that demon-girl Melanie whispers in my ear. "Psst. Do you want to play with my dolly now?" Melanie sounds like she's trying to haul something heavy into my room again. But what's even more terrifying this time is I can't see her. "I brought an even bigger one this time. Pa."

It's too dark!

"*What is happening!*"

I see only darkness. Then I can just make out a dark shadow of my feet on a sheer ledge.

"It's your choice," the stranger's voice says. "Die or be reborn. Do it now. Die in madness or live as magus."

I open my eyes and find myself outside in a large wild grass glade surrounded by the forest. In the center of the wild grass is a bonfire. This is Alondra's backyard. The light from the witches' large bonfire reflects off the surrounding trees. Making the firelight flicker are dancing bodies. A group of women, the girls in our coven, are dancing naked around the fire. Another group is nearby. These scarlet-robed witches are just standing on the other side of the fire, observing. Lucius, that lanky bald man with a goatee, stands in a scarlet robe by the center, watching Alondra's coven dance.

Separating the scarlet group from the dancing naked witches are two large wood planks set in an "x." And tied over the "x" is a pale lady being fucked by a naked man.

I approach slowly. No one seems to notice me. Except Lucius. Lucius turns from the "x" and creepily stares.

The naked woman on the plank moans. This is like the ritual I first witnessed with Alondra on Hilltop Bluff. But Allie promised me she wasn't ever going to do these ceremonies again!

The nude body is being pushed hard against the plank as the man's ass flexes with every thrust. Sweat drips down his body as they fuck each other by the flames.

"Fuck me! Yes, fuck me!"

Alondra's witches start moving faster. They're dancing in three separate circles, small groups of four, before the "x" near the fire, chanting. Their eyes roll back—they seem to be drugged.

"Adramelch! Beleth! Marduk! Paimon! Balam! Belial!"

But the scarlet witches just weirdly stand still, watching.

I hear drums with an increasing tempo, but I don't see the source of the drumbeat. Alondra is the only one in her coven still wearing her black robe, standing by the couple having sex. And beside her is a wood table: an altar with a whip, sword, chalice, and wand. I see something with bloody fur on the altar. And atop the small sacrificed animal is an athame, like the one Melanie was just holding.

Alondra takes the athame in her left hand. That's when I catch sight of her pearly-white eyes. Her lips tremble before the couple having sex. She's drugged and she seems barely able to control herself.

"By this athame, Silvia," mutters Alondra, lifting the knife over her head. She closes her eyes tightly and nods. "We consummate this blessed union. Upon the union of our two circles, manifested by this act, blessed witches, under Selene, you join our groups together, not only with the circle and Ouroboros, but by Jupiter and Saturn. Maga et magus. Magi in unison. By blessed Venus, whose love moves the snake coursing along the tree of life. *Alba et tenebris.* High Priestess and High Priest. Triple Goddess and Cernunnos."

"*Fuck!*" cries the girl. "*Yes, fuck me! Take me! Make love to me!*"

"Drink from this flask, magus," Alondra says calmly to the man. "Drink mandragora and be reborn. Let your energy fill you as it fills each one of us upon this sacred act. May you be initiated with the honor of unifying our two circles under blessed Selene."

Alondra cuts the man's arm. When the man cries out, I recognize his face. It's Bill! My best friend, Bill! Bill is leaning over the wooden "x" screwing Silvia.

Alondra hands Bill a flask, and he gulps down red fluid while still fucking her. As my friend drinks—blood from the sacrificed animal or their drug?—the witches, all the witches in both groups, weirdly gaze up and scream toward the heavens. The heavens answer with a strike of lightning.

"Fuck me!" shouts Silvia. "*Yes! Fuck me! That's it. Join me! Join me under Selene. For our two circles! Join me.*"

But then flickering firelight grows from another direction... From behind me. The witches turn. They seemingly gaze through me. When I turn, I understand that they're not seeing me; they're looking at two witches coming from the house with torches. These witches are wearing forest-green robes. I recognize them as Kenosha and Clotho from the Crescent coven. Both witches in green dip their torches into the fire. But Alondra and Lucius glare. Because, of course, Allie loathes them.

Solus sabbatum. Revelare. Crepusculum. Revelare. Crepusculum in perpetuum.

~

"Don't remove your blindfold."

"Who are you?"

"Bear witness to gnosis by the scarlet whore of Babylon. Tonight, I am in the form of the blessed harlot. Tomorrow, I shall be named Enora, your wife's pupil, bred by darkness. Tonight I initiate you in that darkness as Sophia. Tomorrow, I initiate your daughter, Cadence. Take my master's athame and cut your arm. Cut it, like your little friend did, so that you may be protected from her."

"I don't want to be initiated."

"Cut and drink your blood. The choice is yours over the abyss. Drink and you shall be reborn. No longer of this body. Turn your back on me and the beast takes you. Then you cannot save your wife or Hawthorne. Either by death or change. But the choice shall remain, of course, yours."

But I think I already made my choice. A bloodied athame lies in my left hand.

"Shapeless. Devoid of mystery. Like blessed Choronzon, vying to be seen. Made visible upon all other gods of the occult. A brighter light than night. Plainer than day under the star of Venus. You've already tasted the morning star. Drink so that you will no longer be the observer, but the doer. Allow all acts to be that of God. Drink and you shall be life's creator. For you are my light, Liam. With my gnosis, you can never be harmed, for you are eternal. Your adversaries dwell in darkness. Dwell there for a time so that you may help the abomination see her shadow. Then she cannot harm you. But if you dare turn your back on me, you will surely be struck down. Such it is, that it may consume all light so that you will be blinded by the light of Sophia and never see again. Now drink from my cup so that you may see. Drink."

I shake my head.

"Cut your arm!"

I shake my head again.

"*Cut your arm!*"

There's a bang on the door. Flashes of light spread around the darkness. It jolts my eyes wide open, but that freaks me out more, because I can't see anything behind the cloth.

"Liam, Liam, open the door!" It's Alondra. She's hammering on the door. "What the hell's going on? Unlock this door now! Open the fucking door, Lee!"

I reach over to pull the cloth from my eyes.

"*Do not remove your blindfold!*" demands the stranger.

"I don't want to be initiated. I don't want to be evil."

"You already are," whispers Enora in my ear with a snicker. "Look down at the wound, from the athame, on your right arm, High Priest of Hawthorne. Lick your wounds. Taste the salt. As above, so below. As below, so above. Darkness to light. Light to dark. Circle the flame in your dark firelight."

"*Liam!*"

My body quakes.

"*Liam!*"

The knocking's worse.

"*Liam!*"

It's Alondra.

"*Open the door!*" And her voice breaks. Alondra seems to be crying, fighting back tears.

My eyes are closed, but I *feel* her. How?

She is dressed in her black cloak with a hood over her head, and her fist is raised, ready to rap on the door again.

"*Please, Allie, just stop hitting the door!*"

She hammers it again.

Sparks of light burst across my eyes with her every word or rap on the door. My body shakes with every sound. I just want her to stop talking or hitting or, just...stop doing anything.

"Stop hitting the door. Please."

"Do not remove your blindfold!" demands the stranger.

"Lee!" Alondra snaps. "Liam. God, open the door now!"

I feel a sharp sting in my arm. Looking down, I see a gash with red blood trailing over the white carpet. Weirder, all six candles in my circle are doused out. They must have just been put out, for a faint wisp of smoke emanates from each candle. And yet...if the candles are out, the room should be dark, right? The room isn't dark. From the carpet and ceiling emanates a violet hue, lighting up the whole room.

I scramble up on my feet to switch the light on, but I stumble.

"Is your...ceremony over?" I ask with a shaky voice. "Is... Is Bill still out there? God, I dreamt you initiated him with Silvia? How could you do that, Alondra? You swore to stop all that."

"Liam, that was hours ago. It's four in the morning."

Four in the morning!?

"You keep shouting, babe," Alondra says.

"I'm initiated?"

"Lee, you've been screaming. Open the door!"

"Just stop knocking. Please. Every time you do that, my forehead feels like it's going to explode."

"Execrated," she mutters, mostly to herself.

Through the door, I watch her lift her hand, but, thankfully, she doesn't strike the door again. Instead, she just lays her palm over it.

Wait...how the hell can I see her through the door?

"I thought you were done with sex ceremonies?"

"I already told you why we do the things we do. You didn't let us use your book, so I had to use magic to find the attacker of our hallowed ground. I have to protect my coven, sex magic or not."

But then she falls apart. She starts crying. That's so weird. Allie never cries.

"Mom was attacked by sorcerers from New Haven. Agnes

knows. After Mom died, I found her stuff. I studied tarot, memorized the kabbalah cross, worked sigils, and practiced my shadow work. Later, I found *Broomstick* at the Billington House. Dad tried to stop all of it...but—"

"Allie, why are you telling me all this?"

"I have to explain."

"Who's responsible for attacking us, Alondra?"

But she just cries.

"Allie," I say more softly. "Allie. Who's cursing us now?"

"Me," she mutters quietly. "I'm causing this execration. You have to leave me, Lee. You just have to. It's me... My god, forgive me, Lee. It's me. It's me. I cannot live without you, but...you cannot live with me."

Inhuman screams erupt.

I spin around and see what I've suppressed in my memory for so long. An Ekimmu. A hideous dark, lanky armless figure in pitch-black transparent rags that towers over me, twice the size of a person.

"*Spiritus,*" Alondra whispers by the door. Her voice quakes as if she's terrified. "*Spiritus. Venite foras.*"

"Allie, my right arm is bleeding."

"*Liam!*" Alondra screams in tears. "*Open the fucking door!*"

So I open the door.

There's no one outside in the dark hallway.

"YOUR BLINDFOLD RITUAL IS COMPLETE," THE STRANGER SAYS. "You are initiated and reborn. You are free. You may now be the High Priest of the Hawthorne coven...much better than the next one. You may remove your blindfold."

11

THE DIVINE MASCULINE

Stumbling across the hallway, I land on the doorknob to the bathroom. The walls are uneven, shifting left to right, as if I'm walking in a fun house. I open the door and switch on a way-too-bright yellow light, and my eyes burn. I lift the toilet seat and throw up. Then I gaze through the mirror across from me.

Through the mirror.

Witches surround a bonfire in the backyard, and they are shouting at one another. I'm somehow watching *through* the mirror and walls. I realize this is impossible, but this would be the accurate direction of the backyard. Somehow the mirror is invisible. Is this another hallucination? A dream? I touch my eyes. There's no more blindfold. But is that any better? That means I'm hallucinating.

Alondra looks ready to slug Kenosha across the face. Lucius is shouting at Kenosha and Clotho.

I wash my mouth over the sink.

When I look up again, the wall's back and my view of the backyard has been replaced by our large bathroom mirror. I'm in my bathroom again. My face is made up in the black gothic makeup I never removed. But my hair is frazzled and my skin seems pale. I look so pale. So sick.

Staring, I see right through the glass again.

It looks as if the witches in black and red robes are gathering behind Allie, who looks ready to throw the outsiders out of the yard. That's what her coven did to me last year. They cast a spell to literally toss me out of the yard. Only Billy is far from the bedlam. He is standing near the fire, still naked, untying Silvia from the large wooden "x." Their sick act, or *sacrifice*, must be over.

Slowly I stumble into the dark main hall. As I pass the dining room, I hear utensils clinking against plates.

Are there guests in our dining room?

The long mahogany table is lit in yellow candlelight. Alondra sits in her black cloak, the hood over her head, at the head of the table. Beside her is a young redheaded boy in preppy clothes. This teenager seems far younger than Allie. It's then that I realize that the boy is me when I first met her for dinner at our house last year.

"You asked why we wear gothic makeup and cloaks, and I told you," Alondra says to the boy at the table.

"You lied," he says, shaking his head. "You're not real."

"Get control of yourself, warlock." Alondra turns to me. "None of this is real. Nothing ever was real. All your life is ritual. Nine. Nine. Nine."

The image blurs.

I'm left at a vacant dining room table with shadows of trees through the large window.

Was I drugged? Am I still under the influence? I don't recall taking anything. But I've lost my memory of a lot of things that happened last night.

I touch my face and there's still no blindfold. I must be in deep psychosis now, losing my fucking mind. Like Sister Concezione. *Sister* Concezione... You know something, I never thought of this until now. All the witches in Alondra's coven refer to themselves as *sisters*. Isn't that sinful? It's as if they're "nuns." What sort of nuns? Nuns under the light of Lucifer?

There's more raucousness. Shouts are coming from the backyard again.

I can see the backyard through the walls, and all the witches are still facing Kenosha and Clotho, ready to pummel the green-robed Crescent witches.

I traverse the living room and open the sliding glass door.

Alondra's shouts echo all over the backyard and forest. She's incensed. No...she's not acting like herself. She seems completely out of control. She never acts this crazy. It must be the mandragora. Many of the others look like they're out of their minds too. In fact, I catch Catherine and Nancy slowly wandering by themselves in circles near the bonfire.

Clotho and Kenosha have their hands up, trying to calm Alondra the hell down. They're staring at the bloody athame still in her hand. She seems to have been drugged, and she looks like she could very well stab them.

Beth and Rachel turn and see me. That's followed by a few other witches in scarlet looking over. Beth opens her eyes wide. Under the red-yellow flickering flames from the tall bonfire, her expression is frightening. Beth screams. Other witches scream too.

I look down and realize I'm wearing only underwear. Far worse, my briefs aren't their usual white. They're soaked red. Dark red is caked along my naked arms and chest too. And despite how vivid everything feels, I'm disoriented, as if I'm still wandering in a dream. Weirder, I find that, just like Alondra, I'm holding one of her bloodied ceremonial knives in my left hand.

I feel a sharp sting on my right arm again. That makes me dizzier, forcing me to nearly black out.

"Liam?" asks Kenosha with eyes wide open.

"*Liam!*" cries Alondra. "*My god, Lee! Lee, what the hell happened to you!*"

Alondra forgets all about hating Kenosha and rushes toward me. A whole bunch of witches from both circles run across the wild grass, following her toward me.

Everything turns on its side. Then I see only darkness. But that's comforting, for in darkness, alone with only you and this book, I don't feel sick anymore.

12

CALOR UMBRA

Sun shines through the large floor-to-ceiling window in Alondra's bedroom. It's like one solid brick of golden light searing my eyes. It's way too bright and I have to turn away. What now? I can't take the sunlight? Am I a fucking vampire? What else could go wrong? The light squeezes my head, already aching, making it feel like my forehead is going to explode.

I hear the door open. In walks a witch in a green robe. For a moment, in horror, I fear it's Kenosha. It's not. With her long dark hair and younger features, I recognize Clotho. Clotho sits down on a lounge chair by the window across from Alondra's bed. Then she smiles ruefully.

"Good morning, Liam," she says gently. "Your High Priestess asked that I come and talk to you after last night. Everyone is so worried. And not only your girlfriend, but the witch council wants to find out which witch attacked you. And, well, we know you're weak still but, as with dreams, the time right after the experience is the best time to search your memories."

"I was attacked?"

"Can you identify some of the people you saw in your

vision?" asks Clotho with a nod. "I would like you to tell me every witch that appeared in your dream."

"I...I just hope this isn't a hallucination now."

"I hope I'm not a hallucination too."

We laugh.

Clotho's voice is pleasant enough. She always seems to be. A lot more than her head witch, Kenosha. At first, I thought Clotho looked like Kenosha, but it must be their robes. Clotho's thinner, with less makeup and jewelry.

But then my body shakes all over. And I feel cold.

"*Calor umbra,*" Clotho says quietly, raising her right palm. The words seem to swirl around the room. "*Calor umbra. Calor umbra. Relinquo goetia. Goety. Goety. Goety. Relinquo.*"

Somehow, those words comfort me.

"Who can you identify from your visions, Liam?" asks Clotho calmly. "Whatever you think of us, I'm here to help."

I try to sit up, but I swoon. I touch my right arm—it is covered in bandages.

"Don't move," she says, jumping up. Gently she helps me lie back against my pillow. "Just answer. What witches appeared in your trance? Who did you see? Or hear? To Andromeda and Aurora, their identities are more important than any of the actual events."

"I was casting with *Broomstick.*"

"You've been doing that a lot lately, haven't you?" she asks with a chuckle. "It's okay. I don't know anyone who could resist."

"I...I don't know. I think I was trying to protect myself. But I can't even recall much from late last night, before the ritual. It's like I lost my memory for a couple hours."

"You were attacked. And Kenosha and Lucius believe you initiated yourself in order to shield yourself from dark magic."

"Didn't she kill Lucius?"

"What?" Clotho asks, surprised. She furrows her brow and then shakes her head. "What do you mean?"

"I...I don't know. Nothing."

I shake again. Then I swoon. I lean over.

Clotho grabs a bucket near the bed. I throw up. The bucket was already dirty. Had I thrown up before? After I wipe my mouth with the back of my hand, I fall back in bed.

Then I start shaking all over again.

"*Calor umbra,*" Clotho says quietly. "*Calor umbra. Relinquo goetia. Goety. Goety. Goety. Vade retro goetia.*"

"What are you saying?"

"An incantation to ward off evil demon spirits."

"I'm possessed again?"

"No. You're recovering from a black magic initiation spell."

"That doesn't sound any better."

"You lost blood too," she answers with a chuckle. "When we initiate, we heal the cut made by the athame with magic. You had no such healing spell. But Alondra's athame was a real knife. I think, *physically*, you'll be fine. But mentally and meta-physically, well, you crossed the crossroads. You passed unprepared without any support. You initiated yourself. Some lose their minds doing that. It reminds me of the Abramelin ceremony done alone by practitioners of Thelema. Only, that ceremony takes eighteen months. You did the ritual in one night. Because, we think, you had no choice. If you hadn't done this, a witch was going to kill you. Only by the power of Escoba's grimoire did you protect yourself."

"I was told to cut my arm or die."

She nods.

"And Lucius warned me about being cursed."

"I heard about that," she says pensively. "That's interesting. Willow was convinced that Lucius is trying to harm Alondra's coven, Liam."

I just take a deep breath and shake my head. Then I touch my pounding forehead.

"My head feels like it's going to explode."

"I know this is hard, but it's vital for you and your friend's welfare to tell me everything you can. Who else did you see in a trance? Please name as many witches as you can."

"I saw...the witch of the book. Escoba Hawthorne."

"That's not helpful. A ghost couldn't have cast a curse on you."

"I saw the ceremony in the backyard. I saw my friend's initiation."

"And you probably saw me and Willow fighting Falconsong over that?" She chuckles and nods. "Yes, that unfortunately happened. Any other witches?"

"I can't believe Allie's doing that stuff again."

"Later, Lee. Name all the witches in your dream. We'll deal with Alondra later."

"The girl, Melanie. I saw her. I watched her father fall down the stairs in the house in Geneva Forest. I think she was showing me. I think she cast a spell on her dad to hurt him. But she also keeps asking for my help to fix it. I feel like she's dangerous, but she also needs help. I...I don't know. And then I saw Allie. I fought with her through a closed door. It was all a hallucination, which creeped me out, because she disappeared the moment I opened the door."

"Melanie? The girl from the cursed house near the cemetery? Any others? The council knows nearly every witch in the world. Even a hint can get the headmaster on the right trail."

"Alondra was with me in the living room. But she even told me that it was just another hallucination."

"Never mind Alondra. Who announced your completion of the blindfold spell? Usually a spellcaster, spirit, guardian angel, whatever, helps you cross the abyss and announces themselves."

"There was a stranger's voice. It kept telling me to not remove the blindfold. I think that must have been that witch doing the initiation."

"Did she give you her name?"

"Enora...I think."

"I don't know any witch by that name," Clotho says, furrowing her brow. "But...I think I recall an Enora a couple decades ago in our order." She sighs and shakes her head. "This is so difficult. You could have been scrying time. Crossing into the astral plane causes so much confusion. It must have been terrifying for you. At least when we're initiated, we're warned of all these illusions and our friends are beside us. What about Escoba? Did she tell you why she visited you? That old witch could have left a clue with her book."

"For the sake of our daughters in Hawthorne, she said. What daughter? I'm not sure what—"

I stop talking. Because suddenly Clotho is the one who looks sick.

"What's wrong?"

"What," Clotho blurts, shaking her head vehemently, "nothing. What name did this *daughter* have? Did Escoba say?"

I shake my head. But then my whole body trembles like crazy. I can't... I can't stop...shaking...

"*Calor umbra,*" Clotho says. Her voice is so soothing. "*Calor umbra. Calor umbra. Relinquo goetia. Goety. Goety. Goety. Relinquo.*"

And I wait... The tremor passes.

"Is Alondra still here?"

"It's her house," Clotho quips with a chuckle. "She and Kenosha were up all night examining your book for traces of execration. We've also all been spending hours preparing potions and casting shield spells. Everyone in her coven loves you. You know that. All your friends want to help you now."

"I can't believe Kenosha is even speaking to her."

"For you, yes." She raises a hand. "I have to ask you something very important. You mentioned Lucius. At any time, did Doctor Campbell appear to direct any magic at you? Did it look like he was casting a spell?"

"I don't think so."

"Are you certain?"

My eyes fall on hers. Similar deep brilliant eyes as my girl-friend's seem to penetrate mine. No, more like they penetrate my soul. All these powerful witches—Agnes, Kenosha, Alondra, and now this one—have these mesmerizing eyes. And I feel as if she's not only asking, she's casting a spell to find out.

But she breaks eye contact and turns to the brilliant light from the window. She nods slowly.

Outside, though there's a morning fog, it's too bright for me to look through the window.

"I think I saw Lucius staring at me. But...all of you were. And I can't recall if he was looking at me in my vision or when I appeared to everyone after the initiation."

"Any other witch?"

I shake my head.

"Okay," she says, standing up. "Why don't you get some rest?"

"Can you get Alondra? I want to talk to her."

"When you're stronger, warlock. For now, she really wants you to just sleep."

"Why didn't Alondra ask me all this?"

"I represent the council. And...Falconsong's still a little weak this morning after her ritual. She and many of the others also partook in herbs. Thanks for being such a good sport, Lee. Just rest. The only good news I can tell you is that the ill effects of your initiation spell will wear off soon. You're going to feel better."

"But will I be damned?"

"Huh?" she asks, amused. "What do you mean?"

"Damned. You said it was a black magic spell."

"That's a difficult question," Clotho says with a chuckle.

That's not the answer I was looking for.

"Hmm..." she says pensively. "That's a bit like asking me if you're damned because of all the things you've done before in your life. It's not something I can answer. But I don't believe that engaging in our initiation ritual damns you, in and of itself. I was initiated with the same spell myself and I'm Christian. Many witches in our coven believe in redemption through our Lord, Jesus Christ. But some of us also believe that to be a true witch, one needs to practice left-sided magic to complement the right. No one can tell if you're damned except God, Liam."

I just nod.

"Rest. I think you're still the same good person you were before last night." But as she closes the door, she whispers again, *"Calor umbra. Calor umbra. Relinquo goetia. Goety. Goety. Goety. Relinquo."*

13

———

THE HEADMASTER

I didn't talk to Alondra after that night. In fact, I haven't spoken to her for days. It's killing me. All I did was let her know I needed a break from her—from everything. Then, being totally "Alondraesque," Alondra accompanied me to her front door and just waved goodbye without another word or even a sign of emotion.

But tonight is Friday night. The night of our witch sabbath. So Billy isn't here in his apartment. And I can't—nor do I want to—stop thinking of what my pervert friend is up to again in Alondra's backyard glade. Or what her whole devil-worshipping cult is up to, for that matter. Could they be "sacrificing" another couple on a pentagram? Not talking to Alondra means I didn't get a chance to fight with her over all that stuff again.

I yank off the sheets and roll off the couch.

Well, Liam, there's not going to be any sleeping tonight.

I switch on a table lamp by the couch. In Bill's small studio apartment, it's a bit creepy at this late hour, with just a dim streetlight shining through the one window. I grab my notebook on sensory perception out of my backpack near the couch.

Someone slams their door and the walls shake. That

happens quite often in Bill's little apartment, but this time it is very loud. My neighbors know better.

Then the light switches off. I'm left in shadows.

I'm not alone. In the light, from streetlamps, through the window, I see a little girl in a white dress standing in the middle of the room. It's Melanie! But, much more horrifying, her usual white dress seems to be stained in blood along with her stomach and legs.

Her whole body shakes.

"Melanie?"

She nods. The poor girl seems terrified.

"All gone," she mutters. "All gone."

She looks up and her eyes are pearly white.

"Can't you help us?" she asks. She doesn't look scary, she looks horrified. "Please. Why haven't you brought your book to my house to help ward off all the devils, like I asked?"

Then she shakes her head. No...her whole body quakes.

"Get out!" I shout.

"Me and my friends sure can't let another devil be born here in Hawthorne," she says, almost in a whisper, shaking her head. "We sure can't. You have to understand. But...my friends keep saying they want to meet you. You need to come to my house again. I...I sure can't let no demon be born in Hawthorne. I sure can't." She puts her head in her hands and cries. "Winnie and I have decided she'll have to go. I suppose she's little enough. And then, when I'm through with the baby, do you...do you know, High Priest, what I'm going to have to do to all the other witches in Hawthorne?"

She raises her head, revealing those creepy shiny white eyes again. Then she grimaces: a nasty, devilish grin.

All the lights turn on in the apartment. *All* the lights. The only good thing about that is, thankfully, Melanie vanishes.

The table lamp turns extremely bright. It explodes. Is it the bulb? Then lights all over the apartment light up brightly and explode all along the ceiling, first in the living room, and then in the kitchen, shattering on the cabinets and tile floors. When the bizarre fireworks end, I'm left in complete darkness again. Only the streetlights outside the window light the room.

Now I'm the one shaking.

"Help us, mister," Melanie's voice says, laughing in the darkness. "Please. Please come and help us. Come, let us read your book together."

KNOCK. KNOCK.

My body quakes. There's nothing startling about the sound; it's just that the timing of the knocking freaks me out.

Knock. Knock.

Every knock, like the knocking during my attack at the house two weeks ago, seems to shake my entire body.

Looking through the peephole, I'm hardly reassured. Three women in witch robes with their hoods over their heads are outside on the balcony. One is wearing a brown robe, another light blue, and the other is in forest green. The ones in blue and green I recognize immediately. It's Agnes and Clotho. But I've never seen the young dark-skinned woman in the brown cloak.

"May we come in, Liam?" asks Clotho behind the door. "The witch council wishes to speak with you now."

I throw on my robe and then look through the peephole again.

I open the door.

They all remove the hoods from their heads.

"Bonjour," says the young dark-skinned stranger in her brown robe. She grins. This young witch has a thick accent. She also has a nose ring and many gilded necklaces and bracelets. "Afreyea," she says, tapping her chest and smiling.

"Afreyea has come from very far to help us, warlock," says Agnes, in her British accent. She bows before me. "She lives in Benin near Cotonou. But she is a very powerful sorceress."

Afreyea nods and bows her head. Then Agnes smiles warmly again. "Happy Beltane, warlock. It is good to see you again. I only wish we were meeting under better circumstances. Of course, you know Clotho. She helped you recover from your blindfold spell. And I'm sure you remember me."

Agnes smiles. They're always smiley, even though they all look super creepy in their cloaks. I hug Agnes.

Agnes pats my back and whispers in my ear, "All will work out in the end. Do not worry. I have foreseen it."

I turn to switch on the light, but the switch doesn't work. I guess all the light bulbs were blown out by that demon-girl.

"We should leave the door open for the evening light," suggests Agnes. Then she turns to Afreyea. "Do you still feel her presence here, Aurora?"

"Gone," Afreyea says, shaking her head. But she walks around the room searching every corner of Bill's messy apartment.

"Leave the door open," echoes Clotho. "It will also cleanse the room. Are you all right, Liam? Did she hurt you?"

"Who?"

"The abomination," says Agnes.

"Confusion," echoes Afreyea, looking curiously behind the sofa. "Confusion," she repeats with a nod. "Yes? That's the word, headmaster, you used? Yes?" Then Afreyea turns to me and smiles. "Confusion... Now gone."

"A great confusion indeed, Aurora," says Agnes. "The little girl in Geneva Forest is possessed, Liam. You know your possession by an Ekimmu last year? Well. It was revealed to us at Falconsong's house upon ritual, earlier tonight, that the same demons are now affecting the child in Alabama. Afreyea told us we would find her spirit here tonight. What did the abomination say to you?"

"She said what Afreyea just said. *Gone.* Then she asked me again to come to her house with my book."

Afreyea stops wandering and looks at me, furrowing her

brow. She seems to examine my face and body curiously, as if the girl could be hiding inside of me.

"Liam," Agnes continues, "many in the council believe that Hawthorne is being attacked by the Abaddon Order under Lucius. Because it is unlikely a little girl has the intelligence to cast curses on her own. She is too young. Unless—" Agnes raises a finger. "The demons in that house have imprisoned her astral body and are moving her. That would explain her confusion. But even that event seems unlikely. And unprecedented. I know of no case of a demon possession enhancing the power of a little girl's witchcraft. Actually, the entire situation is...well, unprecedented. But the council and witches all over the world are studying this phenomenon in Hawthorne to try to help you."

Afreyea sure seems to be studying things. She's going about the room picking up keys on a table, sniffing things, all around Bill's messy apartment.

"It is possible that Melanie does not mean you harm," Agnes continues. "She could be reaching out, desperate for help. We just don't know. But we do know now, thanks to Alondra's ceremony earlier tonight upon her hallowed ground, that whatever is empowering that poor little girl, it is Melanie who attacked you on the night of your initiation. You were attacked by that little girl."

I nod. Because I've been telling all of them that all along.

"We have to uncover the rest of the mystery fast," says Clotho. "Afreyea sensed your attack during your coven's sabbath at Alondra's house. She sensed it during ritual. Afreyea is from Benin, Africa, Liam. She is an extremely powerful witch, gifted at birth." She turns and looks at Afreyea. But the brown-robed witch is ignoring Clotho, resuming her search of the apartment. She's going through books on Bill's desk now. "Aurora felt the presence here. That's why we rushed over."

"It's back," Afreyea warns, freezing and standing still.

And that freaks everyone out. Even the witches' expressions

scare me. I mean, these are supposedly powerful witches and they look afraid.

But then Afreyea shrugs, shakes her head, and resumes opening one of Bill's textbooks. "Gone again." And then she laughs.

We all watch her walk over to the kitchen and examine Bill's pot full of old food. Bill has this disgusting habit of cooking in the same pot without cleaning it.

"Are you certain goetia returned, Aurora?" asks Agnes.

"It watches," she says with another shrug. "Confusion watches. Comes and goes. It's funny. Yes?"

"The girl watches?" asks Clotho.

"No." Afreyea shakes her head. "No girl. Goety. Goety watches. No girl. Only devils. Devils watch. But we are...safe. For now." Then she glances at me and squints her eyes. She chuckles. "Only...they really like him."

Well, that's creepy. But then, after making that frightening accusation, she turns away from me and resumes sniffing around Bill's kitchen.

"You've been through so much, Liam," Agnes says with a rueful grin. "The council owes you information—" But then she hesitates. She looks over at Clotho and Clotho nods. "You know Kenosha possessed you to stop Alondra. That was a good intention, but a very wrong thing to do...the council cannot apologize enough."

"I understand, Agnes."

"Yes. Well, I believe that the reason for the present disturbances is Kenosha's witchcraft on that house. The two girls were known to be touching things they shouldn't have even before Kenosha empowered the house. They were already open to shadow magic."

"The headmaster has dealt with hundreds of cases," Clotho adds with a nod. "Your Hawthorne Witch might be known around town as a ghost hunter, but Agnes here is a master at fighting necromancy."

"Goety," Afreyea says with a nod. "Goety."

"What is *goety?*" I ask.

"Goetia," explains Clotho. "Goetia means demonology. Necromancy. Evil black left-handed magic. The home in Geneva Forest was haunted before, but then the High Priestess of my Crescent coven amplified its power."

"Yeah, Kenosha cursed me."

"That's why she isn't here," Clotho says with a chuckle. "And Alondra's absent because she told us you wanted nothing to do with her now. But even if you don't want to talk with them, know that they are working on your behalf to fix all this." She looks down, shaking her head. "Go on, headmaster. Tell him everything."

"It is our fault that you are being attacked," says Agnes plainly with a shrug.

I nod.

"I am sorry, Liam," Agnes says sincerely. "We are so, so sorry."

"It doesn't matter," I say with a sigh. I mean it does, but— "What can be done to stop it? That's what's important."

"Juju," Afreyea says with a nod. Then she grins at me. "Juju. What you do not want, priest."

"What?"

"We must fight witchcraft with witchcraft," Agnes says. "In Benin, *Juju* means magic. Aurora is referring to magic. Only by returning to the house and casting witchcraft, good, right-sided magic, may we fight the girl's curse and stop her demons. With your help, warlock."

"Why do you guys keep calling me a warlock? I'm not. That stupid book just forced me to cut myself with a knife."

"Does it matter?" asks Clotho. "A title won't change who you are. An initiation is only a ceremony. Still, I told you that your life was threatened and only by using magic could you be freed. But really you have been a warlock ever since Kenosha met you."

"We heard you are not speaking with Alondra?" Agnes asks. "I am sorry over that as well."

"Yeah, well, how the hell can *you* be talking to her, Agnes?"

"That tells you how grave our situation has become," Agnes says. "Alondra asked me to come to Hawthorne. Last year was so difficult, but I don't know if you realize that it has been hardest for Alondra. I forgive her, Liam. And, well, Kenosha, they may never forgive each other, but the council needs to help this cursed town. And we need help from you.

"Today, some witches around the world are casting curses against the Abaddon offender, Doctor Campbell. I believe this is a mistake. I do not believe the harm lies with Doctor Lucius Campbell. Kenosha is convinced it does. Perhaps Clotho too?"

Clotho hesitantly shakes her head.

"I am convinced that the true imbalance actually lies with you and Alondra," Agnes continues. Then she raises her palm. "Not intentionally, but through the power of your book, your friends, and Falconsong's leadership. Evil comes from an imbalance, warlock."

"The evil is the girl, Agnes," I say, shaking my head. "I've been telling Alondra that all along. That girl keeps popping up everywhere, freaking me out. She's causing all this trouble."

"But evil imprisons the girl," Agnes says. "It is not just the girl. She is confused. Sure. Liam, you must break your own confusion and know your own guilt in all this so that you may help her. You are in love with a witch. She is in love with you. But she is wicked. So it is logical that the only way you could remain with her was to become wicked yourself. Hence the black magic ritual and the balance of the two columns of magic. And now you even wish to marry her."

"I'm not going to marry her, Agnes," I scoff with a laugh. "I just left her."

Afreyea walks right up to me and examines me. She says, "You are funny too." And then she bursts out laughing in my face.

"In order to fix our sins," Agnes says with a smile. "*All* of our sins, Lee, do not misunderstand me, we are all to blame—we ask that you accompany us to the Grant house in Geneva Forest. Kathy has asked for help. You and the great book's power can be used to help the family. You can help put right the harm we have done. The book is under your power now, warlock."

"You guys are always asking for the book. Why don't you just take it?"

"If it were up to me," Agnes says, "I would burn it."

"Burn it," Afreyea says with a laugh. Then she shakes her head. She walks to the window and gazes outside, "No. Burn, it comes back. You cannot burn the dark. Just as you cannot burn light, headmaster."

"Indeed, Aurora," agrees Agnes. "I cannot destroy the book. We need you to *use* the book, Liam."

"Well, the last thing I ever want to do is go back to that house, Agnes," I reply. "And I'm not too keen on using the book either."

"Things are dire," Agnes says, nodding. "You recall your lover trying to kill me? But, you see, she called for me after what happened to you. The evil manifesting from this prodigy child should never have happened. So many things should never have happened. But they are happening. And..." Agnes looks down. "I sense that the threat extends even further than yourself now. It is my belief that it now extends to the newborn—"

"No," Clotho snaps quickly. "Alondra asked for that not to be told."

"What?" I ask.

"It can't be discussed, Agnes," Clotho says, shaking her head.

Agnes nods her head pensively. But that really angers me. *What are they hiding now!?*

"I thought you guys were going to tell me everything?" I demand.

"Not this, Liam," says Clotho. "This isn't about witchcraft. It's private. Ask her yourself."

"Can you help us, High Priest of Hawthorne?" Agnes asks. "Can you come with us to Alabama with your book? That is also why we are visiting you tonight. You asked to guard the book. The book obeys you, not us. It is under your power, warlock, and we need that power to help the Grant family."

"That freak girl keeps asking me to come with the book. Maybe she's setting a trap."

"I don't see any other way," says Agnes with a shrug. "We need your help and we must go back to the house."

"I was kind of hoping you three came here to help *me*."

"But that is always the way of things, isn't it?" Agnes asks with a chuckle. "The student teaches the teacher. Those in peril save the rescuer. Our world is made of opposites. So says the Emerald Tablet. It is imbalance that leads to danger and evil. We need your help to balance that which is in disorder. Our situation is grave. As I said, all of us are responsible for this great confusion. And so we all need to work together to shine a light in the darkness for Melanie and her family."

"Can you help us, Liam?" asks Clotho.

"Yes."

"The council accepts," Agnes says with a grin. "We will inform you of the time when we shall all meet. But I suggest you make amends with Alondra. Hawthorne is Falconsong's hallowed ground. I must ask for Alondra's help and expect her to accompany us as well."

14

TALKING AGAIN

I'M AT THE FRONT DOOR OF ALONDRA'S HOUSE, FEELING REALLY stupid, knocking on her front door again. Because this is my house. Or...is it still my house? I don't even know. Afreyea and Agnes used the word *confusion.* Yeah, I sure feel confused. My heart is pounding. Sweat is dripping down my back. I don't want to fight with her. I don't know if I want to get back together with her either. But I'm really not here just because the *council,* whatever the hell that is, suggested that I visit her. I came here because of this so-called secret that Clotho made sure to not tell me. And...fuck me, well... I also came just to see her again. Because I miss her. Can any of this be any less *confusing?*

The door opens.

Alondra looks normal, wearing a denim jacket and skirt. She doesn't even have any black gothic makeup on. But she's so scheming that, for a moment, I wonder if her attire is intended to appear "normal" to make up with me. But how would she know I'd be here now? *She's a witch, dummy.*

"Hi," she says solemnly.

"More of your witches came to Bill's apartment. There was another attack on me by—"

"I know about all that," she says, frowning. "I sent for them. Do you want to come inside, Lee? It's not raining anymore, but the wind's cold this morning."

I walk in and take my coat off and hang it on our hook on the door. I'm welcomed by our cat: Sheba jumps into my arms. That makes both Allie and me laugh. Then Allie just walks over to the stairs and sits down on the second step. The chandelier lights are out, but the light from the hallway is bright enough.

"So?" she asks. "How are you making out? I've been so worried about you."

"Upset. Upset over everything."

She nods pensively. Then she gazes down the hallway to the guest room. "Me too."

"The witches said there was a secret you needed to tell me?"

There's a hint, on her lips, of the curl of a smile. Part of me really hates her for that.

"You're in a lot of trouble," Alondra says, turning stern. "You were attacked that night by witchcraft. None of us has ever heard of a witch being initiated to ward off a curse. But that's what happened to you. You were saved by becoming a warlock. Only because of the book."

"I know."

"I know you know. And, whatever happens between us, Liam, I want you to know that I want you safe. That's all that's important. I'll do anything, everything, including working with my enemies, to protect you. I want to do anything I can to help you."

"Three of the witches came to Bill's apartment during your ceremony last sabbath."

"I told you, I sent for them."

"Did they tell you what happened to me that night?"
She shakes her head.

"I saw Melanie again. She appeared at the apartment. That little freak is terrified. Agnes said they think Kenosha empowered the girls when she cursed me. And we think all this harm is coming from Melanie now, not Lucius."

"That night you were sick," Alondra says, "Kenosha thought it could still be Lucius. You should have seen the two of them fighting downstairs when you were sick. But our ceremony points to the girl. It's just so hard to believe. Casting magic needs brains. It's like a little girl doing calculus. It's unheard of. But so is what happened to you, babe."

"You remember Lucius warned me about that night," I say with a nod. "He said I should join you guys in ceremony."

"Yes, I don't believe it's him. And Kenosha's actually helping me cast shield spells for you." Alondra raises her arms in a huff. "I don't know. Everyone I know is helping us, Lee. That leaves only a little demon-possessed-witch girl. Not a really great situation either."

"You think we have to go back to that house in Alabama? Agnes does."

She shrugs.

I creep over and hesitantly sit beside her. She lays her head on my shoulder.

"Oh, Lee," she mutters quietly. "I missed you so much."

"So? What's this secret?"

"Huh?"

"What was this secret the witches hinted at between us?"

That makes her jump up and head to the front door. Somehow, I almost feel like she's going to open the door and walk out. But she stands in the entryway and looks down, just shaking her head.

"Allie, what is it? What the hell's the matter?"

"The worst thing that could happen right now."

"What?"

She takes a deep breath and turns to me. "Whatever happens, babe, everything will work out, okay? If I can keep you safe, know I will. I'll do—"

"What is this damn secret, Alondra?" I insist, jumping up and walking up to her. "Come on. Just tell me for once."

"I'm pregnant." She gazes up into my eyes and frowns again. "I'm pregnant. Sorry, babe. If...if you came to just talk about witchcraft, fine. We'll work to protect you, and we can even split up afterward. But I have to tell you that I've decided to keep the baby, whatever happens between us. I'm sorry, Liam, but I'm going to keep my baby no matter what. I don't want to have an abortion. But, hey, I'm strong. And if...need be, I'll raise our baby alone. I'm fine with that too. Truly I am. I'll love her no matter what."

I feel dizzy. Almost sick.

"Are you okay?" she asks, actually chuckling. Then she searches my eyes.

No. I'm really not.

"Didn't we use protection?"

"Mostly," she says. "I felt cramping, so I checked a pregnancy test."

"When?"

"Last month."

"You were hurting? Did you see a doctor?"

"Liam, I don't believe in doctors," she says. "I'm a witch, a'ight?" Then she shakes her head again. "I don't think you'll ever understand that. I checked again a couple days ago. Yep. Still pregnant. Yippee and congrats. We're having a baby, my darling."

"You're sure it's ours?"

"Don't you go there," she says, growing a dangerous smile.

"I want to help you, Alondra."

"Some pair we are," she says, looking down and shaking her head. "A mom unfit to be a mother and a father that doesn't want a child."

"Who said I don't want a child?"

She doesn't answer. She just looks up derisively.

"If you want to keep her, I want to help you with our baby, Alondra."

"I don't need anyone's help. But...as miserable as we are now, you and me, you need help from my magic. There's a powerful force and it seems to be after you again."

"Now I get it. Melanie kept mentioning a daughter. So did Escoba. No, Alondra, I don't agree. These problems are one and the same. Melanie isn't only threatening me, she's threatening our baby now."

"*Problems*," she says, pensively nodding her head and sighing. "Yes, I suppose a little tyke would sure be a *problem* for me and you."

"Allie," I force my arms around her. "I didn't mean it that way. It's not *a problem*. I'm just shocked. So...you knew about the baby before I left?"

"I didn't think it was the best time to tell you." She gently pushes me away. "Guess I couldn't find the right time."

"I want to be her father."

"You are her father. But...I don't know." She runs her hands through her hair. "I'm not even certain that the baby will be a she? Maybe she'll be a wonderful man, like you? I've tried to predict it, but the future is uncertain. Just like—"

"I love you, Alondra."

"I love you too, Liam. So? Isn't it awful?"

I shake my head. Then I put my arms around her again. But I don't feel happy. And she's right, as she often is. It's just all too much and even in her arms, I feel horrible.

I think another person would cry in my arms now. Not Alondra. I don't think I've ever seen her cry, except in my freak hallucination. Sure, she could take care of a baby alone. She could run a whole family on her own. She already does, with her coven. But that doesn't mean she doesn't need me. And now, with all our other *problems*?

"Whatever happens, babe," she says quietly, "I'll always love you, Liam. Always. I care about you more than anyone."

~

WE'RE MAKING LOVE. SLOWLY, CAREFULLY, BUT WITHOUT A condom. I suppose neither of us sees a point now. But it's wonderful. Somehow, having given each other the silent treatment for so long culminated in this wonderful moment together where, really, just holding one another would have been just as amazing as the sex itself. But the sex is better than before. Because it's make-up sex, always a weird, amazing thing.

She's moaning as I push slowly into her.

Gazing for a moment over my shoulder, I look out the large bedroom window. It's dark outside. Still windy. I can hear the trees in the woods swaying.

I run my hand along the curves of her breasts and soft skin. Then my fingers glide along her leg and around her ass. I squeeze as I thrust into her again, hearing her groan even more. Then she grasps my back, pushing me harder into her. And over and over, closer and closer.

"I think we should get married," I blurt.

"What?" she asks with a chuckle.

"I think we should get married. I want to marry you. Do you want to marry me, Alondra?"

"Are you crazy, Liam?"

"We love each other. Isn't that what normal people do?"

"Yeah, but...we're not normal."

I laugh. Then she grasps me harder. Her lips run along mine, and I feel her explore my tongue. Then she blows air at me as I thrust again.

"Will you marry me, Alondra?"

"Because I'm pregnant?"

"Because I love you."

"*Yes.* That's it. Just like that. Oh, yes! *Yes! Fuck! I love you so fucking much!*"

And she collapses under me. But then she does something

strange, something she always does after climaxing when we make love. She wraps her arms around me, holding me as if she's terrified of losing me.

"Did you mean...*yes*," I ask, panting. "Or...was that just passion?"

"I meant yes," she says, kissing my lips again. "Of course I'll marry you. You're the love of my life. I will never love anyone else. Sure, I'll marry you. But I think you're totally crazy to want to marry me. How do you want to do it? In a church?"

I laugh.

"Is there a witch way?" I ask.

"We do a handfasting."

"I don't think your Uncle Hanley would like that pagan stuff."

"No." She laughs. "Dad would want a church. Is there a church in Hawthorne?"

"Yes, Alondra," I say sarcastically with a laugh, "there's a church in Hawthorne."

"Then we can bring the girls. They can all wear black cloaks and thick black makeup. And Dad can watch his daughter, all in white, walk down the aisle under his god. You can bring your mom, and I'll finally get to meet Lee's mommy."

She laughs. But then she loses her smile as she stares into my eyes and runs her fingers through my hair. With only the light of the full moon shining through the large window, I watch as those beautiful eyes gaze deeply into mine.

"Oh, it doesn't matter, baby," she whispers, shaking her head. "As long as we're together. Alondra Johansen, eh? I really like the sound of that."

15

THE STRANGER

ALLIE AND I AWAKE TO A POUNDING ON OUR FRONT DOOR. IT'S still dark outside with a heavy fog covering the trees and misting the grass. The fog is brightened by the rising sun. And the wind's dying down. I don't hear it rushing against the window. I check the nightstand by Allie's bed. It says it's only seven in the morning.

Bang. Bang.

More pounding. Alondra stirs but then falls to her side, closing her eyes again.

I drag myself out of bed, throw on my jeans, and rush down the stairs.

Bang. Bang.

Outside, through the peephole, I see a thin girl with long blond hair wearing a turquoise sweater and black pants. She keeps looking behind her.

I jump when I recognize her as she turns back to the door. It's Silvia, looking absolutely terrified. This is the same Silvia who helped *initiate* Bill the night of my initiation ritual. She's always so bubbly and happy-go-lucky. Not now. Right now, she looks totally freaked out.

When I unlock and open the door, she leaps into my arms.

"Oh, Lee!"

"What's going on?" Alondra mumbles sleepily from behind me. She's standing at the top of the stairs.

"The doctor's dead! My god, the doctor's dead! He's dead!" And Silvia falls apart, sobbing in my arms. *"Lumi's fucking dead!"* Silvia screams between sobs. *"My god, he's dead, Lee! He's gone! And...you know what? You know what...you...you guys are, like..."* Silvia looks up the stairway, pushing herself out of my arms, with her eyes growing wide. "You guys are, like, in *sooo* much trouble. Cline and Kurt think it's all your fault. Those two never trusted your coven. They all hate witches. I told them I didn't believe it. I met you guys. You guys are so cool. But... God, Lumi's fucking dead, Lee! Our god is really dead! Lumi was amazing. I can't believe it! I feel so bad. And we're all scared. But many, like half our order, are ready to come down to Hawthorne and kill all of you. They want to curse all of you witches. You know, I told you—I respect witches, but members of our order think all witch covens are full of losers. They always have."

"How did he die?" asks Alondra. She sounds so calm amid Silvia's raving.

"He was—" She wipes her eyes. "It was during his private ritual in our backyard. A witch did it, Falconsong. Maybe from the Crescent coven, if it wasn't you. Some witch did it. That's for sure."

"Kenosha's annoying as hell," Alondra says, walking downstairs. "But she's not a murderer."

"Well, this witch wasn't wearing a green robe," Silvia says. "The New Orleans coven wears green, right? This little freak was in one of your black robes. And it was a little girl, we think. She was—" She puts her head in her hands, shaking her head vehemently. "Fuck, I can't get over it! I just can't. But...I mean, we saw voodoo stuff lying around the patio where he died. There was a bloody dead chicken with its head severed. And a small bag full of smelly stuff. And two sticks laid over him tied together in a cross. That's all voodoo witchcraft, right? We wouldn't know. But it seems like voodoo magic.

"Cline saw a little girl wandering around the backyard of the house that morning. Like a little girl in a black witch robe. She must have struck during the night with the full moon, you know, perfect for you guys' witchcraft, worshipping Selene. But I don't know, Cline said it was a little girl in one of you guys' robes. But how could a little girl fucking kill the doctor!

"I mean, my god, Liam! Our god was so powerful. But she killed OUR GOD!"

She shakes her head and falls back in my arms again.

"Fucking Lumi's dead!" she cries in my arms. *"He died!* Can you believe it? What are we going to do? You met him. He's so wise and intelligent and loving. He loved all of us. I loved him more than anyone.

"He was so nice to me, to Cline, Darbie, Mitch, Terry, everyone in our gang. The doctor got me out of such heavy shit in my life. He was the one who, like out of everyone, saved me. And he knew everything—like, absolutely everything in the whole universe. He could help anyone in their path past the abyss. So...how could he be gone?"

Alondra gently pulls her off me and smiles at her.

"Come inside, Silvia," Allie says gently.

She puts an arm around her and leads the sobbing girl into our living room. In the living room I plop down on a chair next to the sliding glass door while Silvia falls on the couch. Then Allie heads back into the hall. I hear a faucet from the sink in the kitchen.

Silvia keeps shaking with her head in her hands.

"I didn't come to cry," Silvia says, shaking her head. She pulls out a tissue from her pants pocket. "I came to warn you guys. My friends are already casting curses. We have Kurt and Cline, and they're very powerful in Thelema. And, boy, they're pissed. The only solution they can think of is cursing you. The coroner is saying the doctor died from a heart attack. He thinks drugs. We know better. It was voodoo witchcraft. I mean, he was dabbling in that too, so it's possible he was adding it to his personal ritual. I don't know. Of course, Cline totally wants to hurt Kenosha and her coven too. Is there anyone in your order that could have done it? Anybody? Do you know about a little girl? She seemed to be wearing one of you guys' robes."

I hesitate. Because of course I know. Then her eyes open wide.

"It's that freak, isn't it! That's the little girl you guys have been hunting in Alabama, or something. You guys named her in ceremony. It was... *Mel*... Melanie's the name, right? What more do you know about her, Liam? I think Falconsong told Lucius stuff, but barely any of us, even me, know much about this little witch. My order's going to try to hurt you guys if you don't tell me everything. Both your covens, 'cause, at this point, well, they don't care who they fucking attack. They hate all witches. They always have."

"It wasn't our coven, Silvia."

"I get that. Because it's this little freak, right? I shouted at Cline a million times, telling her it wasn't you. But you know how much of a bitch she is. I know your High Priestess would never do this. Cline just claimed I'm defending you 'cause... well you know what I did with your friend— "She wipes her eyes with the back of her hand. "But you guys know so much about us now. We let you inside a lot of our private rituals already. We opened up to you when Lumi came to help out. That means you'd know just how to reach and cast curses on us too. But you know, Lee, Cline isn't crying like me right now, that bitch is plotting. And boy, she's a dangerous, sneaky bitch. I used to like her, you know, when I first came to the order. But I actually think she's gone rotten. She's all quiet, but she's fucking nuts inside her brain, you know. And there's nothing worse than someone who's private on the outside while busy plotting nutso curses on the inside."

Ah, yeah. That's not good.

Alondra walks over and hands Silvia a cup of tea. She sips it with shaky hands.

"We'll talk to your circle, Silvia," Alondra says. "All will be all right."

"No! No! Don't do that. Don't you dare do that, Alondra. Not now. No one's gonna listen to you right now. Don't you guys get it? Some witch just cut the head off our order. Kill Lumi and she killed us. That's like the total symbolism of that voodoo-hoodoo bloody chicken head, right? We don't work like you guys. You get rid of the head magus of our order, and you've got nothing left. We're not unified like your witch covens."

Silvia vehemently shakes her head. Then she puts the cup down on the coffee table and throws her head in her hands. *"God! God!"* And she's back to bawling. *"He's dead!"*

"You said a girl?" asks Alondra gently. "A little girl was seen attacking Lucius?"

"Melanie," I say.

Alondra turns to me and quickly shakes her head.

"Cline saw a weird little girl standing over Lumi's body," replies Silvia, "but then she disappeared. The little girl was wearing one of your black cloaks. At times she seemed transparent like a ghost in the morning, and then she was seen again leaning over his dead body."

"Melanie," I repeat.

"We have to work together and take care of this brat fast," Silvia says with a nod. "Otherwise there's going to be war between us. What witch do you guys think is possessing or controlling Melanie? What can I tell my order, after they calm the fuck down?"

"No one's possessing her," I say. "She is a powerful little witch in her own right. But why would she kill their leader, Allie?"

"No little girl could kill our god," Silvia says, shaking her head. "Impossible. I can't believe it."

"If it actually was Melanie," Alondra drawls pensively,

"killing Lucius pits us against their order. If that girl is this much of a prodigy...this genius, and she wants to hurt us, having us war against the Abaddon Order hurts Hawthorne. But that's adult plotting from a little girl casting so-called adult witchcraft—a little girl practicing black magic and scrying with the ability to reach and kill a powerful wizard who's been practicing for over thirty years. That's a lot to attribute to a girl."

"But why wouldn't Melanie go after you?" I ask. "Or Kenosha?"

"It's not as easy to kill the leader of a witch coven," Alondra replies pensively. "We practice in groups. Lucius is easier. He was probably on drugs." She turns to Silvia. "Right, Silvia? He wouldn't have been clear in the head. He might have been able to travel better, scry better, but not focus his intent if he was high. Mandrake, henbane, and nightshade enhance Hecate's power. But Lucius practices alone with substances. I'm assuming he was taking drugs, Silvia?"

"Probably coke." Silvia actually laughs. "Our god always wanted to act like good ole Aleister Crowley. Lumi fucking loved all of his books, especially *Cocaine*. He started to experiment with other shit too. Smack. Acid. DMT. Yeah, that's what the coroner thinks stopped his heart."

"Silvia," Alondra says, "can you call your friends? If you don't want me to talk to them, tell them this had nothing to do with us. Tell him that it was the other witch that we're investigating. Tell them the witch council plans to visit this evil witch and make things right. It's the witch Lucius was helping us fight. The witch is not even, probably, connected with the Crescent—"

"They're not listening to me, Falconsong," she says. "I already told them it wasn't you. You united with us in ceremony. They know that I'm going to side with you."

"You have to try. The witch council is here in Hawthorne right now. I summoned some powerful witches from around the world after the night Lee was mysteriously initiated. I'll work with those witches, but you have to tell your friends that it wasn't the Hawthorne coven that attacked him. Liam and I plan to go back to Geneva Forest. That house has to be the source of our trouble. Somehow a little girl is causing our problems. A prodigy child. I've never heard of such a thing, but she was powerful enough to attack Lucius. Powerful enough to kill him. The answer lies back in that haunted house. But...God, if you're right, Silvia, then this little monster just murdered someone."

"I'll go with you guys," Silvia says. "Sure, after..." She pauses, running her hand through her long hair. "After I call Cline again. I'll need to use your phone here. But...I don't want to call her. She's supposedly my friend. Supposedly. But she's out of her fucking mind now, I tell you. She's not mourning, she's scheming. Maybe if we can prove someone else did this to Lumi, they'll leave you guys alone. Sure, Falconsong, I can come along."

"Ask Cline to just give us the weekend. Just till Tuesday. Just a couple days. The council was going to prepare in another week, but I think time is only making this worse. You go with us and report back, if Cline trusts you at all now."

"Hmm," Silvia says. She shakes her head and runs her hands through her long blond hair. "Maybe. But I hate to tell you, even if this witch is just a little girl, my order is going to hurt her. They're going to cast vengeance on the little brat for what she just did. And they won't care if some other force was moving her to murder him. They're going to want to kill her."

16

HER SHADOW

TREES BLUR ALONG A NARROW, WINDING ROAD. IT'S LIKE A thousand trees flickering golden-yellow rays of sunlight, but behind such beauty shadows lurk amid all the tree trunks and branches. It feels creepy, as if those two little girls are watching me. Maybe they are? If Melanie is so powerful that she can conjure spells from another state and kill the leader of an entire order, or threaten my life in Alondra's house during a witch ritual, would it take much to imagine her watching our caravan near her house? Large leaves cover a wet road and glow under the sun's rays. Though the clear sky is blue now, there must have been a storm yesterday. Beautiful? Could be. Right now, I don't care.

It's quiet. All I hear is the swishing of windshield wipers in my red Camaro, wiping away a light drizzle. I turned off Metallica. It's heavy metal Allie and I both love, but Alondra's studying. I just wish she weren't reading my book, *Broomstick.*

Trailing behind us is Kenosha's old blue station wagon. I can just make out Kenosha in the driver's seat with Clotho as a passenger. And behind that is a gray Ford Taurus rental car.

Alondra's fighting constantly with Kenosha now. First the

two witches were willing to work together to help me on the night of my assault; now they're working together with the mutual goal of protecting Hawthorne. Still, Clotho seems to be tagging along just to keep the two of them from killing each other.

Silvia is driving the Taurus, and Afreyea and Agnes are also in the car. Yep, we're a caravan of witches. And though I'm scared as hell, I feel good in a way with all this magical support. More importantly, I feel like after all these months of hell, we're finally doing something about it.

I hear Alondra turn a page.

"I love you."

"That's random, Liam," she says with a grin. She doesn't look up from my book. "But okay." Her face is decked out in the same thick black gothic makeup as mine. "I love you to death," she says absentmindedly, still reading. "Forever...and ever."

"What'cha reading from that damned book?"

"An ancient rite for exorcising demons. It's Escoba dabbling with goetia. It's interesting how this voodoo witch from Louisiana was working with magic from the *Lesser Key of Solomon*. She was quite a witch. She knew a lot more than local voodoo in Louisiana. But I hardly think drawing a few sigils and circles and sprinkling salt and sage is going to take care of that little freak."

"We'll be there soon."

"Sure."

She sounds as thrilled as I do. Then she kicks back in her seat, turning another page.

"What do you guys want me to do when I get there?" I ask. "No one ever told me how to use the book."

"The magic lies within you. Learning spells fine tunes your magic, but all of us are magi within. The headmaster believes the book alone is a talisman powerful enough to help."

"Help or stop?"

"Hmm?" She furrows her brow and glances up at me. "What do you mean?"

"This girl killed Lucius, Allie. Are we coming back to the house to help? Or to stop her?"

"I don't know." She heaves a sigh. "I just don't know, Liam. But she's just a little girl."

We arrive before that death-defying creaky, narrow bridge. I hate this thing. It's a narrow wooden bridge over a raging river. And it's not really the bridge itself that bothers me; it's the fact that crossing this bridge means that we're almost at Winona's cursed home.

I inch my car along the narrow, creaky bridge.

The clouds seem to provide more shade as I return to the main road. The dead marsh and dense trees grow blacker. Shadows shade us. It's then that I remember it was right here where I wanted to turn around last time.

At the crest of a hill, I see the familiar red and white house. My stomach rumbles. The last thing in the world I ever wanted to do was return here. But the odd thing is, with that driveway, that Ford Bronco and pickup parked near a trash can, a bird soaring above the modern tiled roof, and windows reflecting the midday sun, everything looks absolutely "normal."

It doesn't feel normal.

"What is this feeling, Allie?"

"Evil," Alondra says, staring at the view. "We've come to the right place. Clotho said Kathy's been taking Melanie to doctors. Melanie's been to the hospital, been through blood tests, scans, and, of course, medicine isn't telling them a thing. Because it's not a disease, it's goetia. She's the one possessed by a demon this time, not you. You were right all along about her." She turns to me and forces a smile. "I couldn't believe it, but a little girl is actually hurting us by casting witchcraft."

"I never wanted to be right."

She nods. Then she hands me the book and rummages through the stuff in the back of the car.

I force open the car door.

Our accompanying witches are climbing out of their cars behind us. They put on their witch cloaks. Then they, too, stare at the "normal" scene.

Alondra hands me a black robe.

"What do you see, headmaster?" Kenosha asks Agnes.

"I see nothing, Willow," Agnes says, staring. "I only feel."

"Confusion," Afreyea says with a nod. "Yes? Confusion, Andromeda?"

"Indeed, Aurora," replies Agnes, shaking her head. "Great confusion is coming from this house."

Yeah, I feel that too.

A car honks. That makes us all jump. A beat-up gray van rumbles up the leaf-strewn road. I'd know this van anywhere. It's Alondra's ghost hunter team. An overweight older gentleman with thinning hair, a button-down, and slacks jumps out from the driver's side. Raymond. Ray slings a backpack on his shoulder and carries another large bag. Following him is a guy with a long black shirt, messy hair, and bleached jeans. That'd be David. David takes out a bag full of tied wires and a couple cameras.

"Ghost hunters," I comment to the scarlet witch walking up beside me.

"Far out," Silvia replies with a nod.

"Hey, Alondra," hollers David. "What fun do you have in store for us tonight?"

"Thanks for coming, David," Alondra says with a chuckle. "Hi, Ray."

"Sorry we're late," Raymond says. "Man, this place is out in the middle of nowhere. We took a couple wrong turns. Beautiful forest, though." He glances at me, amused. "You still with this guy?"

Ray reaches out to shake my hand, but I put an arm around him.

"I'm a full-fledged witch now," I quip.

"No surprise, hanging with Alondra," David remarks.

David reaches over for a hug too.

"Hello, Raymond," says Kenosha formally.

"Willow," says Raymond. "Blessed be, High Priestess. And Ariel. Witches, some of you know my assistant, David?"

"Are you going to film the house again?" I ask.

"Ray says you got a straight-up demon possession, Alondra?" David asks. "Of course, anything 'round you never disappoints."

"Is the owner allowing us to set up equipment?" Raymond asks Alondra.

"Just cameras," Alondra says, losing her smile. "But this is the real thing, Raymond. Extremely dangerous. We spoke about this house, and I promised to invite you if we returned. This isn't about observing ghosts. A poor girl inside is possessed by a demon. A Sumerian Ekimmu."

"Sounds right out of *The Exorcist*, Alondra," David says with a big grimace.

Silvia chuckles. But she's the only one of us in a witch robe that seems in good spirits.

"We'll take any shot we can get," Raymond says with a nod. "Maybe catch a clip or so on the camcorder. And we'll keep our distance. We're just thrilled to be invited."

"Remember, Ray," Alondra says, raising a finger, "I want you to shoot supernatural phenomena. But you must exclude the paranormal. Do not capture our spellcasting. Any witchcraft must remain secret."

"That's probably not going to be very easy, looking at all of you, but...sure. It's your show, Alondra."

And that's when all greetings end. Because Raymond and David finally turn their attention toward the house. They look freaked out too. What is it about the place? It looks ordinary enough. But it's like what Agnes said. It's the way it *feels*, not looks.

I hear birdsong. A calm breeze rustles through surrounding trees.

But Afreyea bobs her head up and down in the hood of her brown robe, muttering a foreign language. And Clotho is tying a string around a small bag.

Alondra's the first to step forward. Then the whole group of robed witches follows her onto the small cement porch before the front door.

It turns dark. Clouds occlude the remaining sunlight, and it grows as dark as night. I shiver. It's a sudden frigid breeze. But the cold air leaves as soon as it arrives.

"Are you all right, Lee?" Alondra asks.

"I felt something really cold."

"Juju," Afreyea says to me with a nod. "You feel the Juju of devils, priest."

Oh, great.

Raymond quickly takes some weird device from his bag and holds it in front of the front door. Then Afreyea closes her eyes, bobs her head up and down, and weirdly places her right palm before the door.

Alondra just knocks.

The door swings open. And that, like the car honking, makes us all jump again.

I gasp. Upon the threshold, Kathy, Melanie's mother, has long disheveled brown hair with streaks of white and a very thin and lanky body, as if she hasn't eaten for days. I think she's lost a hundred pounds since last time we were here. And her body's trembling. Behind her, all the lights are off in the house and it's dark. But strangest of all, it looks like someone is camping out in the entryway. There's a sleeping bag, a suitcase, and clothes piled by the door.

"Thanks for coming," Kathy mutters. "Thanks...thanks for coming." Then she turns to Kenosha. "It's worse. It's getting worse and the priest couldn't help us."

"I'm so sorry, Kathy," Kenosha says.

Kathy nods but then oddly puts a finger to her lips.

"How's Mitch?" Alondra asks.

Kathy's sunken-in eyes bulge. "No. No." She whirls around, gazing over her shoulder. "Don't say that."

"We've come here to help, Mrs. Grant," Agnes says calmly. In all this tension, her calmness seems jarring. "I am the leader of the Selene Coven from England. I am the headmaster of the Witch Council and represent the leading witches of the entire world. Your troubles have caught the interest of practitioners everywhere. Be comforted that we are here to cast spells to protect you." I hear children laugh. "We are here to do what we can to help your girls."

Afreyea weirdly sticks her nose up and sniffs the air like an animal. Then she recoils as if smelling something putrid.

"Come in," Kathy says with a hesitant nod. "Come in. It's... it's worse. It's worse than before. The priest couldn't help us. And, I think...it's... because of what happened. Just, please, don't ask what you asked. Don't. God, I haven't moved from here in days. It's so that, if I have to, I can still get out. The girls can, you see—" She looks up at the ceiling. "Hear. Somehow, they hear everything. Even a whisper."

Girls laugh again. Kathy squirms.

Alondra puts an arm around Kathy, but it makes her jump.

"I'm so sorry, Kathy," Allie says.

"It's you," Kathy says with a nod. "It's you."

Crash!

Something from upstairs shatters, followed by the sound of the girls bursting into more laughter than ever. Then there's a tearing sound within the walls. I hear a lion growl. My memory of all this madness makes me want to leave the house and run.

"Do you see anything, witch?" Agnes asks.

I assume Agnes is asking one of the witches. But her bright sapphire blue eyes are staring into mine.

"Do you feel the cold again?" Agnes asks me. "Or do you see a vision? Hold your book close to your heart and reveal what you feel to the council. Your talisman will aid in divination. By sound? By feeling? Goety in this house reached out to you by the door. Do Ekimmu say anything to you through your book now?"

~

I SEE AN IMAGE OF KENOSHA PINNED TO THE WALL UPSIDE-DOWN, a few feet from the floor, in the girls' bedroom upstairs. Alondra lies crouched in a ball, with her robe around her, on the carpet in the center of the room.

"Windstorm. This I breathe. Hawthorne witch. Wait for the next one. And leave me, Lee. It's me. It's me."

~

THERE'S MORE CHILDREN'S LAUGHTER.

"What do you see?" Agnes asks, still searching my eyes with her hypnotic bright sapphires. Her eyes, like those of Clotho and Alondra, seem to pierce right through my soul. "Keep your book close to your heart. If anything else is revealed, tell the council." She turns back to Kathy. "Now please, Mrs. Grant, may we see your daughter? I would like to talk to Melanie."

We follow Kathy through a dark hallway. It smells stale, almost moldy, as if we're walking underground in a cave. Silvia tries a light switch in the hallway—a sensible thing to do—but it doesn't switch anything on. And although the sun isn't down, it's very dark through the corridors.

I notice the living room past the stairs. But Kathy yanks Alondra's arm back before we can enter.

"No!" Kathy warns. "No. She doesn't let us enter without her permission. You must ask her first. You can't go in unless she allows it. This is her favorite place. She's probably playing with one of her dolls."

"Allow me to enter and speak with her, Mrs. Grant," says

Agnes quietly with a kind smile. "I would like you to accompany me, Liam. You have been used as a vessel and mirror for the girl over the past few months. And you, Alondra, should come with him. The love between you can strengthen Hawthorne's bond. You may also serve as protection for our novice. But I believe the rest of you should stay back until the witch council permits your presence."

The other witches hardly argue.

I catch David and Raymond setting up equipment behind me in the dark by an outlet farther down the hallway. David looks frustrated because, of course, nothing he plugs in is working.

Alondra and I accompany Agnes into the dark living room.

Upon crossing the threshold into the room, I'm met with a repugnant stench. It reeks of blood, rotten meat, and feces. But strangest of all, I smelled only staleness before.

There's a large window to the backyard near a sitting area, but the yellow drapes are drawn closed. Between two chairs is a couch against the wall and a brown lounge chair closer to the window. A fireplace is on the opposite side of the room. But much of the furniture, including the large dining table and chairs in the adjoining dining room, are gone. Replacing it is a very large open space with a mess of dolls and toys and paper and old food wrappers strewn around on the white carpet. The adjoining kitchen is even more of a pig sty, with trash piled on the counters and many of the cabinets left ajar.

With gray clouds occluding the sunlight outside, and it turning twilight, it's as dark as night in the house now. The flickering firelight casts fiery shadows on the walls.

We're not alone.

Sitting motionless before the fireplace near their worn-out brown couch sits a little girl, cross-legged in a thin white dress. Her long dark hair is unkempt. And the flickering flames reflect off her small dirty face as she stares into the fire. She seems to be whispering. Under the girl are torn pieces of carpet cut into the distinctive shape of a five-pointed star. Beside the girl is a glass, stick, and knife. The knife is bloody and looks like a ceremonial athame. There's liquid in the glass. It's red. *Is it blood?* Beside the glass is what looks like a piece of animal flesh. Whatever the carcass is, it's unrecognizable.

Alondra gasps.

But she's not looking at Melanie, she's gazing at the lounge chair behind me. There sits a motionless figure, so motionless that I didn't notice him when entering the room. Fire flickers over the profile of his swollen, red-blotched face. Inching forward, I realize that this is Melanie's dad, Mitch. His skin is pale. His eyes are fixed in a dead stare, as if he's another of Melanie's sick dolls. I...I believe he's dead. He must be the source of the stench of bloody flesh. Melanie and Winona's father is dead. Is that why their mother is forbidden to enter?

My God, does Kathy even know?

"May his soul pass safely to inhabit the next body in peace and prosperity," Agnes says quietly over Mitch, gently touching his shoulder. Melanie's body shakes. "Let his soul not remain here in spirit, but pass swiftly to the Summerland." Then Agnes gestures before her body like a priest, but with longer movements and forming shapes other than a simple cross.

"*Walpurgisnacht,*" Melanie mutters eerily with a nod. "*Walpurgisnacht. Walpurgisnacht. Best cover your eyes and ears and try some magic.*"

"Is this Melanie or Winona?" Agnes asks Alondra and me, pointing at the girl by the fire.

"That's Melanie," I answer.

"Melanie," says Agnes, turning to her. "Hello, Melanie, may I talk with you for a moment?" Her sweet tone seems so fake. "My name is Agnes. I am the head witch of the Selene coven in England. I have come all the way from Europe to America to help you, child."

Melanie doesn't answer. She just stares, frozen, into the fire.

Alondra stands by my side. I feel her take my hand and squeeze it tightly.

"Melanie," tries Alondra. "We came here to help you."

Melanie snickers.

"Melanie, they're trying to help you," says another girl's voice. It sounds like it's coming from upstairs.

"I sure don't want any help from the likes of them, Winnie," Melanie says quietly, shaking her head. She continues to stare into the fire. "Nope. Sure don't. Them here is sinners. Momma, what are you doing letting no-good sinners into our house? That's just plain dumb. Stupid and dumb. I'd much rather talk to my friends."

Melanie crouches down, tucking her head close to her chest. She curls herself into a ball, just like Alondra did a moment ago in my vision.

"This girl is casting!" Agnes warns, opening her eyes wide. "Beware, witches. She's using witchcraft. Here is your proof, Falconsong. The young girl is not only possessed, she is a witch casting magic. Witches—"

Agnes is hurled all the way across the house by an invisible force and slammed against the wall in the dining room. I hear screams. But it's not Agnes, or any of us, it sounds like it's within the walls. Then I hear Kathy cry out something incomprehensible.

Melanie looks up and glares at me. Her eyes have turned a pearly white. She grimaces.

The entire house quakes.

"Oh god," Kathy cries from the adjoining hallway. "Oh no, not again."

"No, Kathy," says Kenosha's voice. "Stay outside of the room."

"Melanie, please don't do that to them, sweetie," Kathy says from the outer hallway. "Please. Make it stop. Please make it stop. Don't do that to our guests. They came here to help us."

"There ain't gonna be no silence here among sinners, Momma!"

shouts Melanie. *"No way will I allow that! You know the rules. Why'd you let 'em in without my permission?"*

"I'm sorry," Kathy says in tears. "I'm sorry."

I hear a thousand whispers. The whispers turn into laughter, but the laughter sounds more like the barking of jackals.

Water drips on my face. That is so weird. Allie lets go of my hand and raises her palm, collecting some of the drops. It's as if we're outside and it's drizzling. As if it's raining *inside* the house.

Has a pipe burst upstairs?

Raymond and David shout something in the hallway. That's when the light drizzle becomes a torrential rain. It's as if a bucket has tipped over from above.

"What are you doing, Melanie!" cries Winona. *"You're scaring me again!"*

"Manifest forgotten and lost sinners, Winnie!" shouts Melanie, bursting into laughter. She looks up to the ceiling, her face pelted with rain. *"Arise and spring forth filth! My sun rises, my sun sets. Tiphareth to Malkuth. Malkuth to Tiphareth. Witness the defilement of your daughter by the green devil and three-faced monster, Momma. Upon firelight, witches groping in sinful worship. The evil is you, Alondra! It's always been you, you worthless, wicked, filthy satanic cunt-sucking scarlet whore!"*

Then the freak stares at me again with her all-white eyes.

"Kat-ee Hawthorne," she says derisively. *"Kat-ee Hawthorne. Please, please won't you help me? Kat-ee Hawthorne. Kat-ee Hawthorne, please, please help save me. Please? Please? No! No, no, Momma, there be no saving from sinners digging their fingers in mud, filth, shit, and excrement!"*

"My god, shut her up!" screams Kathy.

"Apage, diabole!" Agnes cries, running back and raising her right hand toward the girl. *"Vade retro! Vade retro! Leave this child!"*

"Walpurgisnacht!" Melanie barks back at Agnes. *"Walpurgisnacht! Walpurgisnacht! Wer glaubt und sich taufen lässt, wird gerettet. Und wer nicht glaubt, wird verurteilt warden! Signa autem*

eos qui crediderint haec sequentur in nomine meo daemonia eicient linguis loquentur novis."

"You asked me to come, Melanie," I shout. The water is falling so hard, I have to cover my eyes. "I'm here. I'm here with the book to help and—"

"Burn 'em witches!" Melanie shouts at me. *"Burn 'em. Burn 'em dry. Suck 'em tender, suck 'em dry. Suck and fuck and watch 'em die. Suck 'em up lean, suck 'em up long! Suck 'em forever drowned in sinner's song."*

Melanie flicks her wrist in my direction...but nothing happens.

"Get out!" Melanie shouts at me. *"Get out of here! Throw your book down and get the hell out!"*

"Stop it, Melanie," cries Winona from upstairs. "He's trying to help you."

"Winona?" shouts Alondra, looking up, "Winona? Are you up there?"

"We came to help you, Winona," I holler, looking up.

The rain stops.

All the lights switch on.

But that makes a bright light shine on this little freak by the fireplace across from her dead father.

Melanie slowly turns back to the fireplace. The water didn't douse the fire. Because, apparently, the water was never here. All traces of rain disappear and it was, apparently, an illusion.

"Help us," Kathy mutters quietly, in tears. "Please. Please help us."

"They be devil-worshipping harlots in my house, Momma," Melanie says, mostly to herself. "Ain't gonna get no help from the likes of them."

"These witches don't want to hurt us," Winona shouts from upstairs. "They're here to help you."

"Shut up, Winnie," Melanie shouts, looking up at the ceiling. "Shut up for once and trust me. No one's gonna be helping your sorry little self."

"Revelare," says Alondra, raising a hand toward Melanie. *"Revelare daemon. Reveal yourselves from this vessel and leave her."*

"Walpurgisnacht!" Melanie snaps at her. Alondra lurches back. *"Walpurgisnacht! Walpurgisnacht!"*

"They're afraid of me, sister," Melanie cries, laughing and gazing up at the ceiling. "They're afraid. Didn't you see 'em shaking by the front door? Just stay in the circle I drew for you upstairs. Sinners can't harm you inside my magic circles. But you can come out, come out, where you are when I tell you the coast is clear."

All the lights switch off again. Only the fireplace continues to flicker with red and yellow flames.

"Melanie," I say in the darkness, "you asked me to come. Didn't you want me to help you?"

"Pray tell," she drawls and nods in the dim firelight. "Pray tell, sinner."

"What happened to your father?" I ask. And I point to the chair.

Melanie turns and furrows her brow. She's calm, but she still has those horrible pearly-white eyes.

She stands up. Even in the darkness, I'm disgusted at the dark stain on her belly and legs. It's light enough by the fire to see that it's old blood.

Melanie stands over her dad, seemingly studying him.

"I think...he's not moving, Liam," she whispers to me. "But —" She puts a finger to her lips. "Momma doesn't want you to know. See, the real secret is—" She puts a finger to her lips again. "Shh. She's already seen him like this. But—" She chuckles. "She just ain't sure. She just doesn't know you, your wife, and your friends the way I do."

"Stop casting spells," I say. "We came here to help you."

She nods.

But Silvia barges into the room. Kenosha and Clotho are trying to tug her back.

"Did you hurt a man in ritual!" Silvia shouts. "A leader of

another order in Carolina? His name was Doctor Lucius Campbell. Did you kill him, Melanie!"

"Yes. My friends knew him. I was there when he died. So?"

"She killed him, Liam!" cries Silvia. "See? This little freak just admitted to it! What more does the monster have to say!"

"*Cum autem perseverarent,*" Melanie snaps. "*Interrogantes eum erexit se et dixit eis qui sine peccato est vestrum primus in illam lapidem mittat!*"

I hear a skirmish. It sounds like Kathy is fighting the witches in the hallway.

"You have to stop this, Melanie," Kathy exclaims, breaking free and barging into the room. "These people came all the way here to help us." Behind her, a little girl in a similar white nightgown with hair just as disheveled runs into the room. That must be Winona. "You have to…"

But her mom sees her dead father sitting in the chair.

"*Oh god!*" Kathy rushes to Mitch, collapsing on her knees. "*Oh, my god! Mitch!*"

Winona stands beside her mom. The girl covers her eyes and starts crying.

"*My god, what have you done!*" Kathy cries. "*What have you done! …What have you done to…your pa?!*"

"Witches, enter the room now!" orders Agnes. "Together we may rid this girl of her possession and help her. Join hands and let us perform—"

"*You dumb did it now!*" shouts Melanie. "*You sure dumb did it good, you stupid witches!* You think a grown woman can handle the death of her husband? Well, now all of you are gonna get it. Now I'm getting mad!"

But Kathy's inconsolable. And everyone has their eyes on her.

"My god, someone take Kathy and Winona out of the room!" cries Alondra.

"Help her out of the room," says Agnes. "Please. Clotho, please help her mom and sister out of the room now."

"You know the rules!" Melanie shouts. "I don't want none of your crying and crying and crying and crying and crying all over my torn blessed carpet. Stop all your crying or you're gonna get it good from Pa."

Then she laughs.

"Please take...them out of the room, Kenosha," Agnes says. "Please, Clotho. This is so horrible."

"Why, is it something a grown woman like you, *headmaster*, can't handle?" Melanie asks, turning to Agnes. "Something too *evil*, angel?"

Agnes's eyes widen. Then she squints at the girl.

"Too much darkness for the kindest leader of sinners of the entire world?"

"What possesses you, child?" Agnes asks. "Who speaks through you?"

"I don't know what you're talking about. I'm just a little girl."

"Who, or what, moves you, child? Show the council so that I may help you."

"You seem well liked enough," Melanie replies. "With your sweet heart. Ain't you the leader of sinners? Pray tell. Pray tell. But how can you show love to people while dancing around the fire naked? Witches be sinners. You talk flowery like God and Jesus about love, but then you do such dirty things. Would you like to see my friends, Agnes? Is that what you want? Maybe if you come and see my dear friends, you won't be so smiley...

"Now, all you witches, this be my house. So it is my hallowed ground. I'll be the one asking questions. Headmaster, or one of you sinners, name the witch who sent a curse down upon my family. Name her and then, maybe, just maybe, I'll permit you, Agnes, to meet these dear loveliest friends of mine."

"Possessor, whatever power you hold in this child," Agnes says, waving her palm before the girl and closing her eyes. "The power of good shall prevail. *Lux alba.* White light occludes darkness. Show me, child, your possessor. So that I may heal you."

"You fucking bitch!" Melanie screams up at her. *"You're not really so nice, are you? Ignoring me? Name the witch! Name the witch you protect. Name the one who cursed my family, and then I'll let you see my sweet, nice heartwarming friends!"*

But then, despite her raging, Melanie cocks back her head at me. She grins.

"Agnes," I warn, "don't agree to anything with this thing."

"Yes, show me your shadow, child," Agnes says. "Show me your *friends*. Liam, this poor girl needs my help. Yes, Melanie, show me your possessor so that I may help take them away from you."

"I ask, you ask," Melanie replies. "You ignore, I ignore. Do you think I am just a stupid little girl? Do you think I don't understand the filthy words coming from your wicked forked serpent tongue? Why don't we play a different game, then. Shall we, Andromeda?"

Melanie raises her right palm toward Agnes.

"Resurgo. Resurgo. Resurgo!"

Agnes's body is lifted into the air. The blue-robed witch hovers, kicking, over the empty dining room. High above the ground, circling over Melanie, Agnes starts pushing off the ceiling, struggling to fall back down.

"Leave her alone!" screams Kenosha.

All the witches are in the room staring hopelessly at Agnes. Clotho takes out one of her small brown bags and raises it toward Agnes. Silvia charges at Melanie, but she's thrown back by some invisible force.

"My god, stop it!" I cry.

"Ain't she funny, momma?" Melanie shouts, laughing. *"Huh? Ain't she funny looking?* Hey, now, don't you be covering your eyes. Come on over and see! Come on. What the hell's the matter with you, Ma? Come back in the room, you hear? This is my magic trick. I'm the one doing this. Not them. Whatcha

think, Winnie? Why, we've got the head sinner of witches flying around on her broom in our living room!"

"Stop it, Melanie," Kathy says quietly. *"Please! Leave the nice woman alone."*

"Blessed be, Momma!" Melanie shouts, nodding her head. "Blessed be."

Melanie drops her right hand. That sends Agnes plummeting to the ground. Silvia, Clotho, and Kenosha rush to her side.

"Walpurgisnacht," Melanie shouts at the surrounding witches. *"Walpurgisnacht, Walpurgisnacht.* As the doctor springs forth a lily flower, the palest white, watch my red blood soak down into the roots as it spills onto you. There be no peace for the wicked. No peace for any of you at all." She leans over Agnes on the ground with those sick all-white eyes. "You want to see my friends, so-called leader of sinners? Go on. Open your eyes. I wasn't gonna do it, but you refused to tell me which witch attacked us. So...you can only blame yourself."

"Goetia. Goetia. Goetia!"

Agnes lets out a high-pitched scream. Coming from such a calm person, it's terrifying.

Her eyes bulge, looking around the room, as if in a fit of madness. Then she curls into a ball against the wall trying to cover her eyes and ears with her arms. But none of us recognizes what she's seeing.

"Do you like 'em?" Melanie shouts, laughing again. "Huh? Aww, what's the matter? Ain't this what you kept asking for?"

"God, stop it, Melanie!" I shout. *"Stop it!"*

"Name the witch that cursed my home," Melanie orders Agnes, standing over her. But Agnes keeps desperately trying to cover her face. "Name her. Name the one who hurt us. Or turn your head and open your eyes. You may look upon my friends instead, if that is your wish. Or...you can tell me who cursed my house. Is it one of the witches watching you fly on your broom tonight?"

But Agnes continues to cover her head.

"Aww, what's the matter?" Melanie says, looking down at her. "Just name the cursed witch and I can hide my friends. Is the witch here right now? Hmm? Was it *you*?"

Agnes shakes her head. Then she mumbles with her whole body trembling, "*Vade retro. Vade retro daemon.*"

"*Verlassen!*" Melanie barks back. "*Verlassen! Damön verlassen! Nien! Nien! Nien!*"

Agnes is hurled against the wall again.

"We all are responsible...Melanie," mutters Agnes, still desperately shielding her eyes. "All of us. I am sorry. We are all to blame. I am so sorry for what we have done to you."

"*Liar! Only one witch casted the spell!*"

"*My god, leave her alone!*" I shout.

Melanie cocks her head back and squints at me. But then she whirls back on Agnes, shaking her head vehemently.

"*Name the one who casted a curse on this house! Name her now, or so help me...!*"

Agnes is lifted up and slammed once more against the wall.

"*Name her! Name the witch now! I warn you. Name her, or else!*"

"It was me, Melanie!" cries Kenosha. "Please, god, please leave her alone. I'm sorry. I was the one who cursed this house. But I did it to stop Alondra."

Melanie turns and stares at Kenosha. She shakes her head.

"*No, Auntie Kenosha's nice!*" objects Winona, rushing back into the room. "No, please, don't sacrifice her, Melanie. Please. Please don't sacrifice her! Auntie Kenosha is our friend."

"Auntie Kenosha?" drawls Melanie. "Auntie Kenosha?" She shakes her head and rubs her eyes. "You made a pact with all my friends? But...aren't *you* my friend?"

"*Auntie Kenosha's nice!*" cries Winona. "*Leave her alone, Melanie!*"

"It was me." Kenosha nods. "I cursed your family and this house."

"But...why?"

"To stop Alondra. To stop the harm she was doing with her evil witchcraft."

"Walpurgisnacht," Melanie says quietly. *"Walpurgisnacht.* I'm so sorry then. Why...it seems I'm going to have to hurt you *and* that witch Alondra."

She raises her right hand toward Kenosha.

"No, Melanie!" cries Winona.

"Cast jumbee under the cross!" Clotho blurts quickly, standing in front of Kenosha, blocking the girl. "Jumbee, by the blessed cross of Jesus Christ, I cast you down, demon. By the power of our Lord Jesus Christ, upon Escoba's own grimoire, her own faith in God, I ask that the demons leave this poor child."

Melanie is thrown to the ground.

"Hey, don't hurt my sister!" Winona yells at Clotho.

"Grab hands, witches," commands Agnes weakly, rising. "Release this Azazel. I command you, demons. Release this child. Relinquish Azazel. This girl doesn't deserve this pain. None of the people in this house do. Show this poor girl our mercy."

The witches circle around Melanie.

"Ain't this *my* house?" Melanie asks, looking up at them, still with those horrid white eyes. "Don't you call your house your *hallowed ground*? Pray tell. Pray tell. You here to curse me and my family some more? Haven't you witches done enough?"

"Relinquo!" Alondra says, gesturing with her right hand toward Melanie. *"Relinquo. Vade retro, Ekimmu. Release your Azazel."*

"Azazel, Alondra?" asks Melanie, whirling around to her. "Azazel? I see only one sacrifice before me, Falconsong. Only one sacrifice in this room, and it isn't me. Nor is it my sister, Winnie. Nor is it Pa, nor is it Ma. Nor is it any other weak little thing in this room. I only see one small, weak thing, Alondra, with a tiny little heart beating deep in your nasty, dark, filthy, disgusting worm-ridden belly."

Alondra drops to the ground near the couch clutching her stomach.

"Don't touch her!"

I fall beside Allie. All the witches huddle beside Alondra now. Allie writhes on the ground in pain, still clutching her stomach. Kenosha and Clotho sit on their knees beside us.

Melanie disgustingly laughs.

"Stop it, Melanie!"

"It's not the girl, it's her possession, Liam," Agnes says. "You must stop, Melanie. Please, witches, no one harm her. I have seen her demons. They're everywhere in this cursed home. Only with love can we help her. Only with love, not anger."

"Stop!" I shout at Melanie. *"Stop it now!"*

"Sacrificium!" Melanie shouts back at me, laughing. She raises her right palm over Alondra. *"Sacrificium! Enteritus en sanguim et..."*

Alondra screams.

"Stop!"

My shouting hurls the wicked girl to the ground again. She rolls across the carpet until she hits the wall in the empty dining room. And whatever I did, thankfully, stops Alondra's groaning.

But Allie looks so weak.

I kneel and hold Alondra in my arms, squeezing her tightly.

"First a child in her belly," Melanie says, getting up. "Then, by my rite, Auntie Kenosha. And then, I think I'm going to kill you, you filthy, disgusting man. *Sacrificium! Enteritus en sanguim! Et completes! Amen!*"

Alondra screams.

"Lee, you can hurt her!" cries Silvia. "You moved her with the magic of the book. It might be her hallowed ground, but you still have the power of the book. You can hurt her back!"

"No, that is not the way, Silvia," Agnes says.

"What happened to your father!" I shout. I squeeze Allie's

hand, looking up at the little beast. God, Alondra grasps back so weakly. *"Is this the same kind of spell you used to kill him?"*

"What?" Melanie asks.

"You showed me," I rage, "in a vision how your father died. He fell down the stairs. You made him fall by casting a spell. Your dad fell down the stairs due to your magic, Melanie. He died because of your magic. Not because of your friends. Not because of Kenosha. Not because of Alondra. Not because of any of the witches. *You* are responsible for your father's death."

"No, Liam," warns Agnes.

"Your witches brought devils into my home!" screams Melanie.

"We came here to help you," I reply, shaking my head. "You asked me to come to the house with my book and help you. But I see there's no helping. You enjoy hurting the woman I love."

Melanie looks confused. Whatever possessed her and spoke through her before, now, after my scolding, she seems to be turning back into a bewildered little girl. Is it the power of my book?

I hold my book up with two hands before her, and it lights up the dark room.

"Demons, reveal your shadow. By the power of Escoba's book, let this girl see what surrounds her. Let her see what she's done. What she is. Show her shadow. Just like she showed Agnes."

"No, Liam!" cries Agnes again. *"I forbid you to harm this little girl!"*

But who the hell's harming who? Alondra is moaning on the floor!

Melanie backs up against the wall again. She opens her lips but says nothing.

But then, the white of her eyes fades. The power of my book seems to be working!

"Don't hurt my sister!" shouts Winona under me, tugging at my cloak.

"Show the child her demons," I cry. I hold the book aloft

again before Melanie. "Show her shadow. *Revelare.* Let her see the shadow she just showed our headmaster. Let her see who helped her kill her own father. *By her own hand!*"

"*You killed him!*" Melanie cries. "*All you witches here hurt my pa! Just as I will hurt you!*"

But Melanie's body quakes. She's looking scared.

"It was you, not us," I reply, "that made your father fall down the stairs and die!"

"*No, it was you!*" she yells. But her voice now sounds like a little girl's. "*All you witches ever do is hurt us! You hurt Mommy and you hurt my daddy! And I hate all of you. You are bad and I want you to get out of my house! Go! Get out of here! Leave our house and leave me and my sister alone!*"

"And what do you think you are? Scrying with flames? Cursing and killing a man? Showing devils to the headmaster? What did you show me by the bottom of the stairs, Melanie? No witch has to initiate you. You're already initiated. You're a witch, Melanie!"

"Stop this, Liam!" warns Agnes again. "She is only a little girl. Her mind cannot take what you're doing to her. It is only with love—"

Love? Love!? Alondra's still clutching her belly.

I jump up and charge the girl. She falls back and hits the wall again, lurching back from me, her whole body shaking.

"*I watched you cut yourself under the stairs!*" I shout. "*Didn't you do that? Didn't you show that to me!*" The girl shakes her head, staring up at me wide-eyed. "You initiated yourself! You hate witches? What do you think you are now? Didn't I watch you cut yourself with a ceremonial knife? Well, you made me a witch. Now I'll return the favor. You've already anointed yourself in blood. What is left? I call upon you, I will initiate you, as a witch." I hold the book before her. Light shines forth. "*Manifesta, Abaddon Maga Completus.* You, Melanie Grant, are a witch, the most vile witch there ever was. A child murderer! You killed a man and you killed your father. Love or hate yourself, either way, keep away from us. Keep far away from Hawthorne. Leave Alondra and me alone. *Stay far from Hawthorne and leave my friends and the Hawthorne coven alone! Manifesta, Abaddon Maga. Manifesta. Abaddon Maga. Penitus. Penitus. Penitus.*"

The yellow glow emanating from my book shines forth, lighting the entire room. It flashes before Melanie's eyes, making her shield her face.

"Recite the words, Lee," Alondra says weakly. "Recite the words of demons. Bring them back to her so she can see them again."

"No, Falconsong!" warns Agnes. *"She cannot take it!"*

"Goetia," Allie says weakly. "Use our book like a black mirror. Repeat...the words three times to cast the spell... *Goetia.*"

"Goetia," I say.

Alondra nods.

"Goetia. Goetia. Goetia."

All the lights in the house switch on.

Melanie backs up until she hits her back against the wall over and over again. But this little girl is not backing away from witches, which normally would be horrifying enough. She seems to be seeing something far worse. Looking frantically about her in a panic, her brown eyes are wide, and her whole body is shaking. She's staring everywhere as if invisible monsters in some nightmare are surrounding her.

"No," Melanie says. "No. Please." Her whole body shakes. "Please. Please, go. Go away. Get them away from me. Get them away. Go away. Momma, please help me! Momma. Daddy? Please. Help me. Please."

"I hate you, Melanie!" Winona screams at her. *"Because you killed my daddy!"*

Melanie keeps desperately pushing herself against the wall. What could be so terrifying?

But that's when I see it. A group of tall, lanky spirits in tattered black cloaks circle around her. They are, oddly, perfectly lifeless. The demons are faceless but have shiny, glowing white eyes. These are the Ekimmu demons I saw last year—a vision I hoped to never see again. They surround the girl. Motionless, doing nothing. But they don't have to move to terrify a child. And then, worse, all emit a scream, the loudest shrill I've ever heard. The cry of the banshee. Melanie covers her ears with trembling hands. So do I. But all the other witches, even Agnes, stare down at the little girl, confused. For I don't think they see or hear her demons.

But I do.

17

———

WALPURGIS

"*Walpurgisnacht!*" Winona screams at her sister. "*Walpurgisnacht!*" Melanie is on the floor shielding her eyes, her head tucked into her chest, covering her ears, with her body shaking. She's covering her head, just like Agnes was. "*Walpurgisnacht.* You killed Daddy! *Goetia! Goetia! Goetia! You did this to us! You killed Pa!*"

Melanie looks up to the ceiling and screams. And with her cry, a thousand other screams come from the walls of the house. This time, everyone hears the anguish, covering their ears.

Melanie looks so pained. But no one moves to console her. The hell if I will. Still, despite the blood on her white clothes, she seems like a normal kid. Her eyes aren't white. They're just full of tears. And even after being terrorized by her, watching a little girl suffer like this is awful.

"*Keep her away from us!*" cries Winona. "*Mommy, keep Melanie away! Please, Auntie Kenosha. Please keep this monster away from me!*"

"*Shut up, Winnie!*" Melanie cries. "*Shut up! I hate you and I hate Momma!*"

I grab Alondra and help carry her out of the room. Then

my eyes stray where I wish they hadn't—to their dead father, still sitting in the chair, staring blankly ahead of him. This part of Melanie's haunting was no spell or illusion.

Cracks form in the walls. I had seen these cracks during the last haunting, but I thought they had been repaired. Now they're reappearing everywhere, all over the walls of the house. Perhaps they had never left?

Then the whole house quakes again.

"Momma, keep this witch away from me!" cries Winona.

"I ain't no witch, Winona!"

Raymond and David are quickly grabbing all the equipment in the hallway. They abandon some wires. They don't care. They want to get the hell out of the house too.

We all do. We rush to the front door.

I wave my hand before the door, and it is thrown open. Then we all rush outside.

Outside it's twilight and quiet. But near the threshold of the front door, I turn. Because Kenosha and Clotho are trying to drag us back.

"Liam, we can't go," Kenosha says, shaking her head vehemently. "We can't leave Winona and her mom. God, even Melanie needs help. She's just a little girl."

"She's not a little girl anymore."

"Lee's right," says Clotho. "That demon is a witch, Willow. And this is her hallowed ground. We can't stop her. But now she's too disturbed to strike back at us. We have to run... Maybe we can return. Just not now."

"What about Winona?" mutters Alondra weakly, held in my arms. "Or, god, her mother, Lee?"

I answer by holding her more tightly in my arms and dragging her farther away from the house.

"Is it over, Liam?" Silvia asks, coming beside me.

How the hell should I know? All I know is we have to run.

We finally stop running when we reach our cars. Raymond and David are already driving off in their van. It's literally as if we ran for our lives. Some powerful witches we are. But, really, I never felt any of us had any control over anything.

"*Walpurgisnacht!*" cries Melanie, sobbing by the front door. "*Walpurgisnacht!*" Her voice is just a little girl's now. But as "normal" as she appears now, we fear the sight of her. "*Walpurgisnacht! Walpurgisnacht! Keep away from here! I warn you! Keep away from my house and stay away from my sister and my momma! Never come back! I hate all of you bad people. Stop hurting us! I hope you all go away! Forever and ever!*"

There's nothing we can do. Nothing. Yet, as I drive down the hillside, Alondra keeps looking back over her shoulder at the house—now not in fear, I think, but in sorrow.

Then Alondra lays her head in her hands and weeps. Tears form in my eyes too. But even as Allie cries, she rubs her belly.

"We had to be safe, Allie," I say, shaking my head. "That's all. We just...had to leave and keep safe."

She nods.

But I still hear Alondra whimpering, even after turning on the headlights, as twilight turns to the darker shade of night.

18

SALEM

ALONDRA'S SUNK INTO A BROWN LEATHER RECLINER SKIMMING through pages of a textbook. Across from her is a couple on the sofa. A guy is rummaging through a bunch of stapled papers while his girlfriend lies asleep by his side. This is our hidden enclave in a sunken-down section of the main library. Nobody knows about the place except eggheads like Allie and me. But that tells you just how busy people are studying for finals during dead week.

"Here you go," I say, handing Alondra a Styrofoam cup of steamy tea. She chose tea over coffee for less caffeine for the baby. "Careful, it's hot."

"Thanks, babe," she says quietly, putting it down on a small table beside her. But then she's right back to heavily focusing on our textbook.

"We really need sleep," I say quietly.

"I know. Just a little longer. I think this might be the first class I fail." She looks up and smiles. "The class I lectured in. How 'bout that?"

"Is your stomach still cramping?"

"No."

"You think he's going to test on that number thirteen stuff you taught?"

I plop back down on the recliner across from her. She doesn't answer, because she's back into heavy studying.

I think it's the third time I got up to refill my cup of coffee. God knows what time it is. Alondra and I have been studying all day and night. If we weren't so behind, due to all our witch problems, we'd have casually studied together at home. But we're so far behind now that we're in full-on focus-in-the-library mode and totally freaked out over our final exam tomorrow.

I open a small book on colonial America. Like Alondra's main textbook, mine is full of orange and yellow highlighting. You know, it's funny. The point of highlighting textbooks is to emphasize particular sentences. I usually just end up coloring the whole thing. Anyway, Dr. Kriegel might not emphasize magic numbers, but he's most definitely going to be talking about Salem.

"I'd remember Ouroboros and the Divine Feminine," Alondra finally answers. "You doing all right, Lee?"

"No," I say with a sigh. "I've got about two more weeks to make up in an hour."

"I was asking more about Geneva Forest and Melanie."

I shake my head. "No...definitely not okay about that either, Allie." But at least I'm doing something tonight to get my mind off it.

Actually, come to think of it, why talk of sleep? I haven't been getting a whole lot of it since returning from that demon house.

"Well, Liam..." She yawns and buries her head in her book again. "We'll have plenty of time to sleep tomorrow."

1692. That might rhyme with *Columbus sailed the ocean blue*—that popular school mnemonic—but it'd be two hundred years after Columbus. 1692 is the date of the Salem, Massachusetts, witch trials. Let's see...nineteen colonists executed, fourteen women and five men, and five prisoners died due to the conditions in a horrible prison. What an awful time to be alive. It kind of makes you appreciate even crazy Hawthorne.

Some point to this clergyman and philosopher named Joseph Glanvill for all the mass hysteria in Salem. Apparently, in *Saducismus Triumphatus*, Glanvill claimed that to deny ghosts and demons was akin to denying one's belief in Christianity and God, and that such nonbelievers in the occult should be labeled as heretics. Ironically, Joseph Glanvill was a puritan who was against religious persecution. So, he was saying one could believe in another religion and be tolerated, but if you were in league with the devil, watch out. He taught religious tolerance while maintaining absolute dogmatism against witchcraft. A subtle difference, but an important one for Puritan America.

I gulp some steamy hot coffee.

Let's see...methods of torture. Well, if you were accused of being a witch, you were often hog-tied and tossed in the water. If you sank, you were believed to be a witch. If you had a noticeable skin blemish, you were a witch. And, speaking of studying, sometimes witches were tested on verses of the Bible in Court. If you got a passage wrong, any part of it, then, you guessed it. You're a witch.

Then there was all the disgusting stuff. Witch bottles. Witch cakes.

Tituba, that famous slave during the Salem witch trials, was accused of baking a witch cake and feeding it to a dog to see if there was a demon in their home. That was a huge mistake. Don't get caught baking witch cakes in colonial Salem, even if it's being done to ward off evil spirits, because then, of course, you're a witch. Fascinatingly, Tituba went missing after the witch trials of Salem. But some say many of the things the slave from Barbados did were part of her culture, part of a different religion, something Glanvill was telling everyone to try tolerating.

A popular way in the seventeenth century to ward off witchcraft was using witch bottles. These disgusting things were made up of a victim's teeth, urine, red wine, and nails. They were buried near one's house or even under a fireplace to ward off demons—kind of like when Alondra buried those small statues of Lamassu in Geneva Forest, Alabama, last year—at Melanie and Winona's demon house.

Stop thinking about it.

I run my fingers through my hair.

Yeah, well...I'm fucked. Not because of Melanie and Alabama. Well, that too. No, I'm screwed tomorrow because these pages aren't splashed yellow or orange with highlighters. Learning all this stuff in one night is not very timely for passing our final.

I jump up and walk to the only really small window in the library. It's mainly for light during the day, I think. Since the room is underground, the window opens up to some plants and the library lawn. It reminds me of a little porthole on a ship. I see the light from a single large streetlamp reflected in the white shroud of an encroaching mist. From this view, I can just make out the back parking lot.

"You're right, maybe we should go?" Alondra mutters with a yawn. "What are you reviewing now?"

"Salem."

"Smart. That'll be on the test for sure. What the hell time is it?"

"Three thirty-three," says the boy across from us.

19

—————

THE HIEROPHANT AND THE
WITCH BOTTLE

"YATU," ALLIE SAYS. THE HOOD OF HER BLACK CLOAK COVERS HER head. She turns to each of us as red and yellow flames flicker over her face. Then she nods at our guests in scarlet robes. "Yatu." She nods at me, beside her, and touches my hand and Bill's. "Yatu, warlocks. Yatu to our guest circle. The Abaddon Order. Blessed be to all friends."

Everyone sends their greetings back to Alondra.

"Blessed be," Alondra repeats with a smile. "May we never thirst. Tonight, under the blessed stars of Astraeus, upon the trees of Cernunnos, by the light of Gaia and the magic of Hecate, we congregate as a united circle. Once more, our two circles meet as one. But tonight is a bittersweet meeting. Tonight, as Liam presides over our coven for the first time, while we celebrate our new leader within our circle, we mourn the loss of another. We can only show our deepest sympathy and regret for the passing of your leader of the Abaddon Order, Doctor Lucius Campbell."

And there is some crying after that.

"Blessed be," I say somberly with a nod.

"Congratulations, bud," Bill says, elbowing my arm.

Because he doesn't know. It's all a lie. The whole plan was

Allie's. Alondra reasoned that, in order to show our guests solidarity and strength, we should come up with the fib that I am now the "Hierophant" of the Hawthorne coven: our Oungan leader or High Priest. Well, you all know what I think about it. There's no way I'm ever going to be the leader of this coven.

"Symbolically we are blessed by fire," Alondra says. "We may be parted by the flames, but we are together in mourning over the passing of your Doctor Lucius Campbell."

Silvia puts her head in her hands.

"Doctor Lucius Campbell was a personal friend," Alondra continues. "Because of the unity he shared with us before he left, we are here tonight to mutually persevere in the face of the challenges in the wheel of life."

"Atman," I say.

"Atman," Alondra says with a nod.

"Please stand, witches," Alondra says.

We all stand.

"*Lux alba,*" Alondra says. Bill adds, "*lux tenebris.*"

"*Lux alba,*" everyone echoes. "*Lux tenebris.*"

"Hail, Satan," Cline says.

"Atman," repeats Alondra.

"Androgyne," Alondra says to Cline across the flames. "In our coven, you would be the same as me, your blessed High Priestess and revealer of mysteries. And so you and your equivalent Hierophant, Kurt, now lead your Abaddon Order." She gestures to Beth, who holds a candle. "Please allow the Hawthorne coven to present this gift. This memorial candle is an offering to you and your order. It is with our prayers that Doctor Campbell has passed swiftly to the Summerland. And we hope that this gift can help make it so."

Beth circles the bonfire. She takes a knee before Cline. Then she offers her a flickering black candle with two hands, reminding me of the way Cline once offered tea to her deceased leader.

"May his soul pass safely to inhabit the next body in peace

and prosperity," Alondra continues, "and let his being pass without being left here in spirit. I and every witch in our coven, including our newest High Priest, wish him a swift journey."

"Atman," I say.

"Atman," say many in our circle.

Alondra looks at me. Because it's my turn to speak. Silvia, though still running the backs of her hands over her eyes, smiles at me under her scarlet hood too.

"We only wish the best between our two groups," I say. I turn mainly to the witches in red across from me. "I deeply respect how much your leader loved our craft. And we, and every witch in Hawthorne, only want love between us. This is not only a memorial service, it's a continued show of friendship. All of you have heard what happened in Alabama. The witches of the council not only possessed me last year, they created a monster. Demons now possess this little girl. And, as witnessed by one of your own members, Silvia, it is this confused girl who killed your leader. And so, we propose we work together—"

"We will deal with the abomination," interjects Kurt, "at the time and place of our own choosing."

"We agreed to come here out of respect for the death of the doctor," says Cline, nodding. "But we never agreed to work with your circle ever again. We respect your efforts. But the pact between us ended with the doctor's death. What happens to the girl, Melanie, shall be decided by us. As I have said many times before, his death shall be avenged."

"Blessed be," Alondra quickly says. She puts a hand on my arm and shakes her head.

"Blessed be," I mutter.

Kurt glares suspiciously at me.

But I'm not about to argue with them. That is the point of our ceremony. Our words are sincere in that we wish for peace. But everyone—though it's unspoken—knows the ceremony isn't about their leader. It's an effort to stop the animosity between us.

I hold back a deep sigh of relief when I see Cline finally accept the candle and stand. She nods to Allie and me. Then she bows with the black candle in both hands.

She lowers it into the large flames, lighting it. And then she sits back down and hands the lit candle to the next member of her group. But I have to look away from her hateful stare.

Each member of her group holds the candle with two hands and lowers their head, some standing, some sitting, in prayer as they pass it around our fire. As it passes a half circle, it finally lands back into the hands of Nancy, one of our coven's witches. She hands it to Beth, and it continues to Cass and Jessica, all the way around until it lands back in Cline's hands.

"The flame will surely burn out," Alondra says with a smile. "But know that upon each re-lighting, you capture a flicker of your teacher's soul. This is his reflection. For Lucius's true brilliance will never fade. Just as his shadow will never disappear. The light of his flame is eternal, and his soul shall never leave us. Friends, he was one of the most—if not the most—brilliant magicians I've ever known in this world. Remember that, though the reflection may fade, his soul, his internal energy, will never leave you."

"Atman," I say.

"Atman," say all of us with a bow.

And with that, we all rise.

Every witch embraces the person next to them, whispering our popular "may you never thirst" or "blessed be" in their neighbors' ears. The other group doesn't take as well to our greetings. A few ignore efforts from my black-robed sisters at hugs. Their order are Satanists, Gnostics, and magicians dabbling in chaos magic. Many hate witches.

"Thanks, Liam," Silvia says, walking over and embracing me. "I think that was wonderful. You guys are so nice."

I pat her back. Then she reaches for Alondra.

"May you never thirst, Silvia," Alondra says with a grin and nod.

"You guys too. May you never thirst, Falconsong."

Then Silvia glances over her shoulder at Kurt and Cline. They still appear hardened and cold.

We watch as their group exits Alondra's backyard and leaves the Hawthorne coven, my coven, alone.

Silvia stays back to talk to me.

"They doubt you're their leader," Silvia says quietly, "and that you've finally taken to her coven. But that's okay. They know what this really was about. At least you tried. I think all you guys are amazing. Take care of yourself, Liam. I know you guys gave it your best shot."

"Bye, Silvia. Thanks for arranging the ceremony with your friends."

"Sure, Liam." She kisses my cheek.

Alondra walks over, watching Silvia exit alone across the side yard of our house. The other black-robed witches from our coven return to the bonfire.

"What did she say to you, Lee?" Alondra asks.

"I don't think we did a thing," I say, shaking my head. "They're hell bent on fighting us. Just as they are on cursing the girl."

"All we can do is try, High Priest."

"They saw through that too, Allie," I say, rolling my eyes.

"Saw through what, babe?" she asks with a smirk.

"Have fun in your ceremony with your friends." I take my robe off and hand it to her. "I'm going to go read in the house while you guys do your thing. You know, Billy actually believed you were making me High Priest."

"Because the title's yours, Lee. It'll always be waiting for you when you change your mind."

20

ALONDRA JOHANSEN

I'M ROCKING TO ABBA AS THE TOTALLY DISCO TUNE BLARES through our large outdoor speakers. It's a bright and perfect sunny summer day. In the woods surrounding the wild dark green grass of our backyard, the sun's rays flicker through leaves stirring in the breeze. It's perfect. Alondra and I chose ABBA especially for the reception, and now we're grooving to "Voulez-Vous," back-to-back, in suits and dresses, laughing, while trying not to spill the champagne from our long-stemmed glasses. Tables surrounding our backyard glade are covered in white tablecloths and decorated with pink ribbons tied around large vases full of lilies, peonies, and roses. Alondra and I are wearing white. I'm in a cool white tux with a tail. Alondra chose this amazing long white dress that flows all the way down to her high-heeled shoes. The heels have brought her nearly up to my height for my thousand kisses. But the wedding party is in black—per Alondra's master plan. Yeah, in a sea of white and green, Rachel, Beth, Jessica, Billy, and the rest of the bunch are all in pitch-black wedding clothes. But we're witches, okay? It was hard enough for them all to avoid wearing black gothic makeup. (Actually, Silvia's wearing black makeup.)

I think I'm dancing where we usually burn our logs for our bonfire. Of course, the logs were cleared from the grass. That'll change soon enough.

And now we're clapping like idiots to the music.

It's a lot of fun.

"Congratulations, honey," says my mom, touching my shoulder. I turn around and she hugs me and kisses my cheek. Then she turns to Alondra and hugs her too. "Congratulations, Alondra. I have to be on my way now."

"Oh, thanks, Ms. Johansen," Alondra says.

"Chrissy," Mom corrects Alondra with a nod. "Call me Chrissy."

"Or...Mom," I quip. "Mom, you're leaving now?"

"We had your wedding cake," she says with a shrug. "Seems it's over and time to go back to Raleigh, Lee."

The song changes to "Summer Night City," another tune by ABBA that Allie and I love.

"Bye, Bill," Mom says, touching Bill's shoulder too.

"Oh...hi, Ms. Johansen," Bill says, stopping his pogoing up and down. "I didn't see you."

"Goodbye," Mom says to Allie and me again. "It was a lovely ceremony at the church. Hawthorne is a really beautiful college. And the manor you and Alondra have here is absolutely wonderful. Like I said in church, I think you two make a lovely couple, and I hope you stay very happy here together."

"Of course, Mom," I say.

"Bye, Liam," Mom says. "Alondra."

"Bye..." Alondra mumbles, "Mom."

"Falconsong!" Rachel says, rushing over. "Hey, Falconsong. We're almost ready!" But then she sees Mom and turns quickly and puts her hand over her lips.

I quickly shake my head.

"Hey, now where do you think you're going, Chrissy?" Uncle Hanley asks, catching my mom by the elbow. "You can't leave. I haven't given my speech yet."

"Oh... I..."

Uncle Hanley laughs joyously.

"Come here," Uncle Hanley says, wrapping his arms around me and Alondra. "Come here...everyone, everybody. Everyone be quiet so you can hear me... Alondra, can you turn down that racket for a sec?"

"Sure, Daddy."

Alondra turns to Rachel and nods. Rachel runs back to the patio.

"And now, well," Uncle Hanley hollers, "hey, where's Reverend Matthews? Where is that incredible man?"

People do their best to give Uncle Hanley space. Uncle Hanley seems even shorter than usual among the sea of dancers. But he's distinctive enough in a casual bowtie, suspenders, and beige suit.

"Right here, Mr. Hanley," our reverend says, raising his hand and dodging his way over.

The music abruptly stops. That makes everyone dancing or standing around by the tables turn.

"Well, everyone, first off," Uncle Hanley says, raising his champagne glass, "I really want to thank Reverend Matthews for making our day so meaningful. That was a blessed ceremony, Reverend. Blessed. Thank you so much for coming to Hawthorne."

"It was an honor to marry your daughter and this nice young man, Mr. Hanley," the reverend says with a nod.

"Yes. Yes. Well, thank you. And as for you, *son*." Uncle Hanley says, putting an arm around me. "Why, you're married now. Right? No time to run. But I feel a bit bad for ya. I really do. You have to deal with all my daughter's antics, which I've had to deal with for so many years."

"Daddy!" Alondra says, smacking his arm.

"Alondra," Uncle Hanley says with a laugh. And he hugs his daughter tight. "You couldn't have done better than with this guy." Then he scratches his head and turns serious. "He has a good heart, a good head on his shoulders, and he's mighty respectful. Why, he even laughs at my jokes. You take care of this wonderful young man, hear?"

"I will, Dad."

"Now you two promise to live with one another till death do you part? You two love each other? Cherish one another? Care for one another? And all that?"

"We will, Uncle Hanley," I say with a nod.

"Yes, Daddy."

"Then I'll be as happy as pie," Uncle Hanley says, opening his hands wide. "Or as happy as a pig in the mud. Good luck to you two and...well everyone, *go back to your fun, hear?*"

"Thanks for coming, everyone," I say to the crowd, putting an arm around Alondra again.

But before Alondra and I can go back to ABBA, Rachel snatches my wrist.

She pulls me aside, opening her eyes wide. "Now, Liam? Huh? Now?"

"Well, I better be heading home myself, Chrissy," says Uncle Hanley. "Bye, Liam. Bye, sweetheart."

I turn to Rachel, smile, and nod. "Now, Rache."

Rachel rushes back to the house, beaming. Then as Allie and I watch our parents leave, I lean into Alondra's ear.

"The girls are getting the stuff ready. It's not over yet, wife."

"Thanks, babe," she says, kissing my cheek.

"I feel happy," I add quietly in her ear. And I squeeze her tight.

"Me too."

And why not? It's a perfect lovely, warm summer evening.

"Hey, Alondra," says a man in a sky-blue suit. At first I have no idea who it is. Then I recognize him standing near Raymond in his suspenders. It's David. I've never seen him in formal clothes. "Congratulations, you two!"

I hug our two ghost hunters.

And then, quietly and discreetly, I make my way out.

I signal to Bill and Beth nearby. Silvia's already at work, lighting all the candles in the yard. We won't see them till the sun goes down. But, boy, when that sun sets, all those candles are going to be absolutely brilliant.

～

"ALONDRA," RACHEL SAYS UNDER THE FLICKERING FIRELIGHT. "Liam. Please face each other."

I'm still wearing a tux and Allie's still in her long white dress.

"We use one ribbon to represent each family. And a final ribbon to symbolize the union creating this marriage. Are you two ready for our handfasting?"

We haven't changed our clothes. But our backyard sure has transformed.

Our bonfire is burning. Candles are everywhere, surrounding the bonfire and illuminating the surrounding trees. And the remaining guests—the ones not averse to pagan ceremony—include every one of our sisters in our coven and even my friend Bill. They are now wearing black robes, standing before us to bear witness to this marriage before our coven's bonfire. Raymond and David are also in the crowd. And I catch Silvia standing behind our coven, wearing one of our black robes.

"I love you, Lee," Alondra says, tears forming in her eyes.

"I love you, Allie," I say, gazing into her eyes. Her mesmerizing perfect green eyes.

She's wearing my necklace. The simple emerald gem necklace glistens in the firelight.

Rachel ties the Celtic cords around both our wrists...with a little difficulty. That makes us laugh. Alondra spent an hour teaching her last week.

"Behold the knot is now...tied," Rachel says. "Finally."

We all laugh.

"Alondra Johansen and Liam Johansen, you are one. Two pillars made one. Blessed be the two of you under Astraeus, Selene, and Gaia. Upon this Earth." She gazes up and nods. "Hecate, witness this bond in Hawthorne. May it never break. Our High Priestess—" Rachel chokes up, brushing tears from her eyes. "Sorry... I'm just so happy for you. Our High Priestess...has finally found her companion. You... Now you two may kiss each other and show your love to our coven, to Hawthorne, and to Hecate. Blessed be, man and wife."

And we kiss. Probably a bit too long.

Some chuckle. Some cry. But everyone applauds.

And that's it. We were married. Twice. Do you think it was sneaky to have a ceremony without our parents? Yeah, well, sure. But how could I respect my witch-wife by only marrying her in a church? My wife is the Hawthorne Witch. It seemed the only way to give respect was to have two ceremonies. And, really, whether it be in a church or in our own backyard, our vows are true.

"I love you, Alondra Johansen," I say. And I bring our tied hands up to my lips and kiss them.

"I love you more, Liam. Forever...and ever more."

THE END

EXCERPT FROM BOOK 3

"CHAPTER 1 - BURN THE WITCH" IN WALPURGIS, BOOK 3 OF THE HAWTHORNE UNIVERSITY WITCH PREQUEL SERIES BY A.L. HAWKE

Walpurgisnacht.

Why did Melanie keep saying that? I can't get the image of the demon-freak out of my head—her creepy all-white eyes, raising her little hands high while grimacing in madness. She kept saying the word for Walpurgis in its original German, *Walpurgisnacht.* She said it so much, it felt almost like a tic. At other times she barked it like a dog.

Walpurgisnacht.

Alone in the main hall of Jonathan Brewster Taylor Library, studying at a long empty wooden table surrounded by the familiar aisles of books, it's always quiet. But this morning it's very quiet. Because everyone's gone home for the summer. There's a stack of books to my right, and a history book opened up discussing the Walpurgis Night. I need to learn everything I can to stop her.

Walpurgis Night is a festival that takes place on the evening of April 30th. It's the day before Hawthorne's better known witch festival: Beltane. Here at Hawthorne, Beltane is a huge ordeal where frat boys drink and dance half-naked, in drunken revelry, with bare-breasted ladies near bonfires. Of course,

Allie's group loves it. But we really never celebrated Walpurgis. I hadn't even heard of Walpurgis until I looked it up.

The two holidays have a lot in common. Beltane is a Celtic ceremony, whereas Walpurgis is German and Scandinavian. The festival of Walpurgis Night, *Walpurgisnacht* in German, celebrates the life of St. Walpurga, a saint who fought illnesses, like rabies and whooping cough, along with—you guessed it— witch curses. Upon this night, people lit bonfires to burn effi- gies of witches. And, like so many other Christian holidays— Christmas, Easter—it's likely that this holiday for the saint was established by the church on a night already celebrated by pagans. After all, Walpurgis Night and Beltane fall celestially between spring equinox and summer solstice. So witches were probably gathering around bonfires on April 30th way before Saint Walpurga was even born. Under Celtic tradition, Beltane heralds the meeting of the three-headed goddess and the green man. The three-headed goddess represents a woman's youth, middle age, and old age. I suppose the green man with horns represents nature. And, like the Greek god Pan, this depiction fits well with the church's hellish imagery of Satan. Walpurgis is different. In Sweden, on Valborg, they sing songs while lighting bonfires. In Germany, they dress up like Halloween, play pranks on people, and cause all sorts of noisy raucousness to scare evil spirits away.

Like so many things I've learned in the occult, Walpurgis is confusing. Walpurgis features villages where witches chant and dance around bonfires on one hillside, while effigies of witches are burned in large pyres on the other. What a creepy mix of witch-love with witch-hate. But that sort of fits Melanie, doesn't it? Melanie wants to use her witchcraft to hunt witches. Still, the creepiest thing to me is that this little demon-girl seemed to perfectly understand the holiday while I had to research it all morning in the library.

"Hello, Liam."

It's a familiar voice. Cline, wearing thick black gothic

lipstick, and her lips and face are emotionless. She's wearing black suspenders over a white T-shirt. Her eyebrows are shaven. A large bald, broad-shouldered man stands beside her. He has a large shaggy blond beard and is wearing all black with purple shades. I recognize him as Kurt, the pale male leader of their cult.

"Ninety-three," Kurt says with a solemn nod.

Whatever the hell that means.

"How is she?" Cline asks, deadpan.

"In a lot of pain," I say, closing the book. "What can I do to save her?"

"Help us kill the girl," replies Cline with a shrug.

"Silvia and I returned to Alabama," Kurt says. "The house was abandoned. You guys called the cops? Well, it wouldn't be surprising if the place was condemned after the body of her father was discovered. And with both girls dabbling in occult witchcraft, they probably were sent to a funny farm. But sanatorium or not, we have to find her. We can use divination. If we do that, you can help. Knowing what she did to our god, she's probably not only after your unborn child, she probably intends on killing your wife. Your wife is, after all, the leader of your order too."

"Melanie hunts witches," I reply.

"Have you been invoking the Ritual of the Pentagram?" asks Cline, nodding.

"And the Lesser Ritual of the Hexagram," I reply with a nod. "Yes, I've studied your rituals."

Cline nods at Kurt with a smile. I think it's one of the only times I've seen her smile.

"We don't have the doctor," Cline says, "but we have you, witch. And we have your book. You cast with your Book of Shadows and lead your coven, and it might be enough to send this abomination into the fire. We propose to summon the girl astrally in your backyard during ceremony. There we can trap her once and for all."

"But can we get rid of the Ekimmu while still leaving the girl unharmed?"

"That girl murdered Luminous!" Kurt rages. "She even killed her own father. Possession or not, Melanie's mind is diseased. Maybe brilliant, but seriously fucked up in the head. And now this little piece of shit is preparing to kill your—"

"Meet me at my house tomorrow for ceremony."

"Does Alondra know about us casting at your house?" Cline asks.

"She's too sick."

TO BE CONTINUED IN WALPURGIS, BOOK 3 OF THE HAWTHORNE UNIVERSITY WITCH PREQUEL SERIES ®

ALSO BY A.L. HAWKE

PARANORMAL ROMANCE

- ALONDRA
- BOOK OF SHADOW
- WALPURGIS

- THE HAWTHORNE UNIVERSITY WITCH SERIES I-III
- THE HAWTHORNE UNIVERSITY WITCH SERIES 4-6
- THE HAWTHORNE UNIVERSITY WITCH HOLIDAY COLLECTION

- SHADES
- HAUNTING JOY
- PHANTOM MASQUERADE

- MY EVIL EYE
- THE GUARDIAN
- NECTAR OF AMBROSIA
- CORA

FANTASY: THE AZURE SERIES

- HARMONIA
- CORA: RISE OF THE FALLEN GODDESS
- AZURE BLUE
- CORAL RED
- PRINCESS SOJOURN

SCIENCE FICTION

- CANDY SAVANT SERIES

Books available at https://alhawke.com/books

PARTING WORDS

What did you think of *Book of Shadow*? By placing a book review, you can inform others of your thoughts and help spread the word about my book.

Want more? Periodically I like to send news regarding current or new projects. If you'd like to be privy, I encourage you to sign up to my email newsletter. Your information will remain private and you can cancel any time.

Sign up at www.alhawke.com or scan the following QR code:

ACKNOWLEDGMENTS

I want to thank George B. for continued support and advice with another beta read. Stephanie Marshall Ward for another invaluable copy edit. Alexa's proofread in polishing another novel. And Brosedesignz cover design's creation of a misty ethereal image—capturing my vision perfectly, as she always does. Finally, a final big thanks to, you, my reader. Your interest in the Hawthorne Witch Series helped push me to delve deeper into the occult and Hawthorne's darker past. That was a lot of fun.

ABOUT THE AUTHOR

A.L. Hawke is the author of the bestselling Hawthorne University Witch series. The author lives in Southern California torching the midnight candle over lovers against a backdrop of machines, nymphs, magic, spice and mayhem. A.L. Hawke writes fantasy and romance spanning four thousand years, from pre-civilization to contemporary and beyond.

Visit A.L. Hawke at www.alhawke.com

Email: contact@alhawke.com